The Lester Affair

A JOAN KAHN BOOK

Books by Andrew Garve

The Lester Affair
The Case of Robert Quarry
The Late Bill Smith
Boomerang
The Ascent of D-13
The Long Short Cut
A Very Quiet Place
Hide and Go Seek
The Ashes of Loda
Frame-up
The Sea Monks
Prisoner's Friend
The House of Soldiers
The Far Sands
The Golden Deed

A Hero for Leanda
The Galloway Case
The Narrow Search
The Megstone Plot
The End of the Track
The Riddle of Sampson
Death and the Sky Above
The Cuckoo Line Affair
By-Line for Murder
A Hole in the Ground
Murder Through the Looking
   Glass
No Tears for Hilda
Fontego's Folly

Andrew Garve

The Lester Affair

HARPER & ROW, PUBLISHERS
New York • Evanston • San Francisco • London

A HARPER NOVEL OF SUSPENSE

THE LESTER AFFAIR. Copyright © 1974 by Andrew Garve. All rights reserved. Printed in the United States of America. No part of this book may be used or reproduced in any manner whatsoever without written permission except in the case of brief quotations embodied in critical articles and reviews. For information address Harper & Row, Publishers, Inc., 10 East 53rd Street, New York, N.Y. 10022.

FIRST U.S. EDITION

Designed by C. Linda Dingler

Library of Congress Cataloging in Publication Data

The Lester affair.

I. Title.
PZ3.W7354Le3   [PR6073.I56]   823'.9'12   73-14313
ISBN 0-06-011456-8

The Lester Affair

SOURCE. Memorandum from William Willis to the Art Editor of the *Star*, a national daily newspaper. Saturday, April 14th.

(Willis, 31, has been a staff photographer on the *Star* for eight years. One of the top men in his field. Winner of 1970 Best Picture Award in national competition. *Ed.*)

As I was going into the Memorial Hall, Paddington, this afternoon to cover Jim Lester's adoption meeting, I was approached on the pavement by an attractive young woman. Apparently she had noticed the press badge I was wearing, and wondered if I could help her. She said she was sorry to bother me, but might I by any chance be talking to Mr. Lester after the meeting was over? I said, "It's possible—why?" She said, "Well, I know it's awful cheek asking you, but would you be kind enough to give him a message? You see, I've been abroad, I only got back yesterday, and I saw in the paper that he was speaking here today, and it seemed a good chance to let him know I was back. But they say it's a ticket-only meeting, just for party members, and they won't let me in."

I was interested, particularly as the girl (25 plus?) was quite an eyeful. I said, "Are you a friend of Mr. Lester's?" And she said, "I suppose you could say that. I met him when he was on holiday in Scotland last year, and we went swimming and sunbathing together." That got me even more interested. I said, "Well, I don't mind trying to give him a message. What's your name, by the way?" She said, "Shirley Holt." I said, "*Miss* Holt?" and she said yes. I asked her where she lived and she said Egerton Road, Surbiton. She added, "That's when I'm not traveling. I'm a children's nurse and I travel a lot." I asked her what the message was, and she said, "Could I scribble a note, it won't take a minute?" She couldn't find any paper to write on, so I gave her a sheet from my notebook. She wrote a few words on it, and folded it and gave it to me, and said she was terribly grateful, and smiled. As she half turned away, I took her picture.

As I say, the note was only folded, and when I got into the hall I glanced at what she'd written. I'm quoting from memory, but the message went something like this:

Dear Jim,

Remember me?—Shirley Holt. I got back from my travels yesterday and tried to come to your meeting but they wouldn't let me in, so I hope this reaches you. I expect you're rather busy but I'd love to see you again if it's convenient. I'm still at Egerton Road. Hoping to hear from you sometime.

Love,
Shirley

When the meeting ended, there was the usual gathering of newsmen round Lester. I took some pictures and waited till the political chat was over and Lester was about to move away, and then I said, "Excuse me, Mr. Lester, but a young lady who couldn't get into your meeting asked me to give you this note," and I passed it to him. He glanced at it, frowned, gave a faint shrug, and slipped it into his pocket. I said, "She was a charming girl, sir, and she said she was a friend of yours. Could we hint at a possible romance?" He gave me an amiable smile and said, "I'm afraid not. As far as I know, I never had the pleasure of meeting the young lady. I think there must be some mistake."

A mistake didn't seem very likely to me, because there was a huge photograph of Lester on a poster outside the hall, with his name on it in large letters, and Miss Holt had pointed to it when she'd first mentioned him. Perhaps there *is* romance in the air, and Lester is holding out on us. The picture of the girl is a honey—couldn't we use it? With a careful caption? If it turns out there's something in it, it could be the scoop of the election.

2

2

SOURCE. Report in the London *Evening Banner*, Saturday, April
14th. From "Our Political Correspondent, Alastair Crewe."

(Crewe, well known for his TV and radio commentaries, has
only recently joined the *Banner*. He is noted for his individual
style of political reporting. The *Banner* gives general support to
the Progressive Party. *Ed.*)

Mr. James Lester was formally adopted as the Progressive Party candi-
date for Paddington South-East at a well-attended meeting of constituency members and party workers this afternoon.

The atmosphere in the hall was gay, almost heady. The scent of
coming victory was unmistakable. The keynote was struck, amid laughter and cheers, when the chairman, Sir John Waldro, recalled that Mr.
Lester had proved to be "a most conscientious Member, working tire-
lessly on the problems of hundreds of his constituents without any
concern for their politics," and added, "We shall no doubt have to make
some allowances for him in the future, as he will probably have heavier
duties elsewhere."

On the platform, Mr. Lester made his usual impressive showing. He
is, as most people now know, a physically attractive man—dark, handsome, and well-built. At forty-four, he gives an impression of youthful
vitality; yet the touch of silver in his sideburns and the surprisingly deep
lines of his face are more reminiscent of the elder statesman. His accent
is of the Cam or the Isis (old style) but his dress verges on the trendy.
He speaks without gesture in a quiet, reasonable, rather reflective tone,
as though he were inviting a dialogue with the voters rather than trying
to force his opinions on them. This style, conscious or unconscious, gives

his speeches a curiously intimate and personal quality. The total effect is one of effortless authority. His words are carefully chosen, his sentences lucid, their content thoughtful. Without a trace of demagoguery, he commands his audience. Undoubtedly he has, in the vogue word of the moment, charisma.

He may well have something more lasting and valuable to contribute to the British political scene. Politics, Thomas Jefferson said, is "a talkative and dubious trade." Talkative it must be; and in the eyes of many people today it is dubious, too, a squalid affair of maneuvers, ambitions, and vicious infighting, of shams and deceptions and downright lies, deserving no respect. James Lester could well give the trade a new image, for what shines out of him is a rare sincerity and candor; an innate, unforced inclination to be honest with his listeners.

Perhaps the most remarkable passage in his brief speech of thanks to the faithful this afternoon was the following, which I quote verbatim with some pleasure:

"Now I'm going to be absolutely frank with you. *(A wry smile.)* Oh, I know that when a politician talks of frankness most voters reach for their lie detectors *(laughter)* and I don't blame them. But when I say frank, I mean frank, and I am speaking now particularly to the young of our party. Our criticism of the outgoing government is not just on account of its policies—though we believe some of its policies to have been misguided, and some to have been folly. Our irrefutable charge is that, after twelve consecutive years of office, this government is tired out, its administration decrepit. If parliamentary democracy is to survive in this country—and heaven help us all if it doesn't—there must always be an alternative government waiting in the wings, ready to take over with new zest, new spirit, and new ideas. We are such an alternative government—and soon we shall be taking over. *(Loud cheers.)* But let us not pretend, to ourselves or to others, that this means that Utopia is just around the corner. The same problems will remain, the same intractable problems—crime and violence, strikes and riots, inflation, unemployment, poverty, housing difficulties. These are part of modern life. If we say we can cure them, no one will believe us—and they will be right. No government can work miracles, no government can do more than its best. But when a government which has been long in power falters, when it drifts helplessly from crisis to crisis, when it seems to have given up hope, that is the time when someone else must take command, a different party, a party of youth and courage and vigor. A party that still has hope. . . ."

It was interesting, as the meeting broke up, to eavesdrop on some of the comments of the dispersing audience. I collected: "breath of fresh air," "That's one for the cynics," "First time I ever heard a politician tell the truth," "unorthodox," and "civilized." One doubter said, "Bit over the heads of some, perhaps." Another asked, "Can he keep the voters roused with that line of talk? They do like to have their villains, you know."

I heard no one say the speech was dull.

3

SOURCE. Linda Tandy's diary. Monday, April 16th.

(Miss Linda Tandy, 26, daughter of Oliver Tandy,
Editor-in-Chief of the national daily, the *Post.* Has been her
father's secretary at the *Post* for about four years. A slender,
vivacious brunette with above-average I.Q. *Ed.*)

The reason I decided to keep this diary over the period of the election was that I seemed to have an exceptionally good seat in the political stalls —what with Noll* ear-to-ground in Fleet Street and knowing practically

---

*Linda Tandy usually called her father "Noll." She explains that she found "Father" too formal, "Daddy" too childish, "Dad" too abbreviated, and "Oliver" too familiar. "Noll" began as a bit of family fun, and lasted. Tandy's closest friends also use this form. *Ed.*

everyone, and James at the very center of the battle—and I thought a day-to-day record from the inside might be of interest—if only to me —after the dust had settled. But a rather upsetting thing happened this morning, so right at the beginning the record becomes personal as well as political, and goodness knows where it will end.

Noll and I were having our usual semi-working breakfast at the flat we share in Hampstead, going through the batch of morning papers to see what stories our rivals had got that the *Post* hadn't, and vice versa. At least, *I* was. Noll was concentrating on the political news and comment in the "heavies," which—judging by his frequent grunts of approval—was much to his liking. And no wonder, with the latest opinion poll showing the Progressive Party in the lead by 25 percentage points and predictably an easy winner. With that sort of margin, it would take an unheard-of last-minute shift of opinion to upset the forecast.

I'd finished with the *Express* and the *Mail*, and picked up the *Star* —and it was then that I got the shock. Across three columns of its front page it carried a photograph of a girl under a bold heading: JIM'S HOLIDAY FRIEND? The text below identified the girl: "Miss Shirley Holt, a children's nurse living in Surbiton, who says she 'swam and sunbathed with her friend Jim Lester' on a Scottish beach after meeting him on holiday last summer. Jim's comment yesterday: 'There must be some mistake. I'm afraid I never had the pleasure of meeting the young lady.' " Beside the main picture there was a small inset of James, from stock, and one of Mary, with the caption "Jim Lester's wife—died tragically after a car crash three years ago."

I sat staring at the page, feeling kind of hollow inside. Presently I passed the paper to Noll. "Here's something that will shake you," I said, trying to sound casual. Noll has never had an inkling, and I didn't want him to have.

He glanced at the picture and read the text, frowning. There was a rather long silence. Then he said, in a phony-tolerant tone that didn't take me in for an instant, "Well, the old dog! So that's what he got up to after I left him."

"He says he didn't," I pointed out. "He says he never met her."

"Mmm . . . That could just be an off-the-cuff denial to the press while he thought it over. Like saying you're 'just good friends' when you're planning to marry." Noll studied the picture again. "She looks an attractive girl, doesn't she?"

I had to agree that she did. The photographer had caught her in half-profile, the face slightly uptilted and smiling. The effect was charming.

"I wouldn't have expected him to be such a fast worker," Noll said.

I was thinking the same thing. James had had only a day or two alone on his boat after Noll had been called away from their holiday cruise together. It didn't seem much time to get to know a girl that well—to be swimming and sunbathing with her. Not for a man as deliberate in his actions as James normally was.

Noll said, a little doubtfully, "I wonder what this will do for his image."

I shared his doubt. "Very little, I should think." The story seemed to me extremely snide, as it was probably intended to be. It was typical of the *Star*, which was a nasty little tabloid and politically very anti-James. Their use of Mary's picture struck me as particularly revolting in the context. James had never really got over Mary's death—at least, I hadn't thought so until now. The picture was unnecessary, and would hurt him. The story, with its innuendos, was distasteful. The whole thing made me feel quite sick.

Noll said, "Well, I'll give him a ring when we get to the office, and find out the strength of it." He was still frowning. "One thing's for sure—the reporters will be buzzing round that girl like flies today."

SOURCE. Memorandum from reporter George Stewart to the News
Editor of the *Daily News*, a national paper. Monday, April 16th.

(Stewart has been with the *News* for many years and is now
one of their senior reporters. He is a persuasive talker with a
sympathetic manner and a benevolent appearance. The *News* is
strongly anti-Lester. *Ed.*)

Fortunately, Shirley Holt has her own telephone, so I was able to get
her address from the directory. I arrived at Egerton Road around eleven-
thirty. Shirley rents a two-room, self-contained furnished flat on the top
floor of No. 37, a three-story Victorian house set in a small garden. She
was out when I arrived and there were at least a dozen reporters and TV
men milling around, trying to find out where she might be from other
tenants. I cast my net a little wider and by the luck of the game found
a woman in a house opposite who said she'd seen Shirley going off just
after ten with a shopping basket, probably to the local supermarket. I
went to the market and prowled around and presently I spotted her. She
was easily recognizable from the picture in the *Star*.

I introduced myself, and asked her if she'd seen the *Star*. She said she
hadn't, so I showed it to her. At first she seemed quite incredulous.
Apparently she hadn't realized she'd been photographed. And the story
shook her even more. She kept saying, "I don't understand—I don't
understand at all. . . ."

I said I was sorry to have upset her, and that she looked as though
she could use a drink, so what about popping into the lounge bar of the
White Lion, which was right opposite, and having a chat over a glass
of something? She didn't say no, so I took her shopping basket and she

tagged along with me in a sort of daze. On the corner by the pub I bought a midday *Standard.*

I settled her in a quiet nook and went to get the drinks, leaving the *Standard* with her. When I rejoined her, she was staring down at the paper and looking more dazed than ever. I said, "Something new?" and she showed me what she'd been reading. There was a brief paragraph on the front page quoting a comment that Jim Lester had apparently made that morning after he'd seen the photograph of her in the *Star:* "This girl is a total stranger to me."

I had the opportunity now to take a good look at Shirley Holt. She's of medium height, very slim, but with an adequate figure. She wears only a little makeup, and doesn't need much. There was nothing noteworthy about her dress, except that it was quiet and suited her. She has smooth fair hair, well-groomed, and an unusually attractive oval face with high cheekbones and green eyes set slightly on the slant. The face isn't particularly lively—in fact, it can become rather expressionless at times —but it has the appeal of a lovely piece of scenery. Her voice is pleasant, educated, with no marked accent. She gives the impression of being, in normal circumstances, a composed, gentle, amiable girl, rather unworldly, and in some matters quite naïve.

To return now to our chat. She put down the *Standard,* looking rather miserable, and said, "Well, that's not very nice, I must say." She was obviously referring to Lester's second and more emphatic disclaimer of any acquaintance with her.

I said, "He seems very positive about it. Isn't it possible you could have mistaken him for someone else? Some other Jim Lester you met?"

She said, "Of course not. Jim isn't a man you could confuse with anyone else. Especially when—" She broke off without finishing the sentence. "It's so humiliating," she said. "I feel terrible. . . . It's not at all what I'd have expected of him—he seemed such a considerate person. . . . I suppose he thinks he's something important now."

I said mildly, "Well, he *is* going to be Prime Minister in about three weeks' time. You can't get much more important than that." ·

9

She stared at me blankly. "Prime Minister! You *are* joking, aren't you?"

"Certainly I'm not joking," I said. "The way the opinion polls are going at the moment, there's absolutely no doubt about it. . . . Where have you been, for heaven's sake?"

"I've been abroad for the past seven months," she said. "First in France and then in Portugal and then in France again. I hardly ever saw an English paper. Anyway, I never read the political stuff."

"But you knew there was going to be a General Election here, surely?"

"Not till I got back on Friday and happened to see a headline. It's not really very interesting, is it? I mean, they're all the same when they get in."

I took a long pull at my tankard. "Well, before we go any further," I said, "I think I ought to bring you up to date with the situation, if it won't bore you too much. Okay?"

She nodded, and I started to explain the position.

"When you met Mr. Lester—in the summer, I think you said—he was a Progressive Member of Parliament. He wasn't very well known in the country as a whole at that time, but he was a rising star in his own party. He was shadow spokesman for something or other, I forget what. Nothing frightfully important. But it did mean that if and when his party formed a government, he'd probably be in the government." I paused to see if I was registering. I rather doubted it, but I plowed on. "Then, during the winter, he got a big boost—he was elected to the Shadow Cabinet. That meant that he was all set to become a Cabinet Minister when his party came to power. Are you with me?"

"I think so," she said. "It's—it's really quite overwhelming. I never dreamed . . ."

"Anyway, that was the position until three weeks ago. Then, with the election just around the corner, the Progressive leader, Arthur Grantley, had a heart attack and dropped dead. You've heard of Grantley, surely?"

"Oh, yes—I remember *his* name."

"Good! Well—then Lester was elected the new leader. The Progressives were in a bit of a spot, you see, because the only people in the party with experience of government, after twelve years of power by the other side, were pretty long in the tooth—and it was a question of choosing one of them or going for the dynamic youngster. Which they did in the end by a narrow margin. I don't happen to be a Lester man myself, but from their point of view there's no doubt it's turned out a first-class decision. The Progressives had a big lead under Grantley—now it's huge. And when they win the election in three weeks' time, Jim Lester will be the new Prime Minister."

Shirley slowly shook her head. "Well—I hardly know what to say. . . . If I'd realized, I certainly wouldn't have bothered him. I'd no idea he was so important. . . . Now I suppose I'll just have to forget about it." Then she added, with a flash of spirit, "All the same, I don't think a man has the right to humiliate a girl in public just because he's going to be Prime Minister. I mean, he ought to set an example, oughtn't he? I suppose he felt a bit guilty. . . ."

That seemed the moment to get her another glass of sherry.

When I'd set the drinks up again, I said, "Would you care to tell me, Miss Holt, just how you came to meet Mr. Lester?"

She hesitated for a moment. Then she gave a little shrug. "I don't see why not. . . . It was near a place called Tobermory, on the Island of Mull, early last September."

"I know Tobermory," I said. "A very picturesque spot . . . Can you remember the exact date, by any chance?"

"I remember it was the day before I left for London. . . . So it must have been—yes, September 5th."

"Good. Sorry to interrupt. Please go on."

"Well, I'd had a job for four weeks with a family from London who'd taken a holiday villa on Mull. There were two small boys, and I'd been looking after them. I get jobs all over the place, you see, mostly through the Franks Domestic Agency, in Kensington—I've been using them for years—or else through recommendations. I get quite a lot of those, too, but this was an agency job. It suits me, changing about and seeing new places, because you never get bored that way. Especially if they're by the seaside—I adore the sea. Well, this had been rather a wearing job, because the boys were a bit troublesome—you know, four and six, not really naughty but very active so you had to watch them all the time—and Mr. and Mrs. Tancred were away a good bit during the day, playing golf. So when the four weeks were over and the family went home, I thought I'd have a day or two on my own in Tobermory and relax before the next job. So I put up at the Island Motel. I didn't have a car but they didn't mind and it was cheaper than the hotels. . . ."

She broke off and took a sip of sherry. I didn't say anything. I didn't want to spoil the flow.

"It was lovely weather," she went on after a moment, "and I lazed and picnicked and explored; it was wonderful. There were a lot of holidaymakers in the town, but I found some quiet places, away from the roads, where they hardly ever came. People just don't like leaving their cars and walking, do they? The day before I was due to leave for my next job, which was in France, the weather was absolutely super. So I took some lunch and a book and a bikini and walked to a little cove, about three miles from Tobermory, which was a bit difficult to reach and quite deserted. The sea was so blue, with hardly a ripple on it—it was heavenly. The only thing in sight was a small yacht, anchored quite a way out.

"Well, I ate my sandwiches and lay in the sun for a while and I was just thinking I'd have a swim when I heard an engine. I sat up and looked out to sea, and there was a little boat coming into the cove from the yacht—a black rubber one, the sort you blow up. It reached the shore, and the man in it pulled it up out of the water and then started to walk quickly up and down the beach, as though he wanted to stretch his legs, and the third time when he passed me he smiled and called 'Hullo' and I called 'Hullo,' and the next time he slowed and came over and we started talking the way people do. He was a most attractive man—really charming, I thought—and presently he sat down and we went on talking."

12

I said, "Can you remember what you talked about?"

Shirley reflected. "Oh, all sorts of things—ourselves mostly. That's what you do when you've just met someone, isn't it? He said he was just coming to the end of a sailing holiday and that he'd had a companion, a man, who'd been called away suddenly because his father was dying. He told me about some of the islands they'd explored together, and what he'd been doing since. I told him what I'd been doing on Mull, and about my jobs and how I liked to move around, and he said hadn't I got a boyfriend and I said nothing you could call serious because I wasn't ready to settle down yet. And he said he'd had a wife but she'd died after an accident. I told him my name, and he said his was Jim Lester, and that he'd started off as a barrister but now was interested in politics. He didn't say anything about being an M.P. and he didn't go into any details about his work, and I didn't ask him because I didn't want to seem inquisitive. But we talked about plenty of other things, and the more we talked the more we seemed to hit it off together.

"By now it was well into the afternoon and the sun was very hot and I said I really must have a swim. He said he wished he could join me, he was quite envious, but he couldn't because his trunks were on the yacht and it hardly seemed worthwhile going all the way out to get them. I said I didn't really mind whether he had trunks or not—well, I mean, men are more or less all alike, aren't they, so what does it matter?—and there was no one else about. He said he'd feel shy if I had a bikini and he had nothing, so I said all right, if it would make him feel better I wouldn't wear anything, either. So that's what we did, and we had a super swim, except that the water was a bit cold, and then we came out and lay on the beach sunbathing."

"Still without clothes?" I asked.

"Well, yes. . . . It doesn't mean a thing after the first couple of minutes, you know—you take it completely for granted. . . . So we started talking again, in an easy, friendly sort of way, and the afternoon wore on, and presently Jim said how about coming out for a drink on his yacht. Well, I'd never been on a yacht, and anyway I liked him, so

I said all right and we dressed—not that he had much to put on, only an old pair of yellow slacks and canvas shoes—and he launched the rubber boat and took me out to the yacht."

I said, "What was the name of his yacht—did you see?"

Shirley gave me a sharpish look. "Now you're trying to check up on me, aren't you? You don't believe what I'm telling you."

"I've a completely open mind," I told her. "It's not my job to believe or disbelieve. I'm just a reporter, gathering and sifting the facts. That's all."

"Well, I don't care," she said, "you can check up as much as you like, because it's all true. But I don't remember the name of the yacht. I know it was stuck up on the side—in black letters, I think—and it was painted in white on the rubber boat, too, but it was a long funny name that just didn't stay in my mind. Sort of foreign."

"I see. . . . Anyway, what was the yacht like?"

"It was white, all white outside, I think. Not all that big—about, say, twenty-five feet or a bit more. I'm not much good at measurements. It had a mast, and red sails that were sort of tied up, and a rather smelly engine, and a big open space at the back where you sit outside, and a cabin with a bunk on each side and a table in the middle, and a gas cooker near the door, and a little compartment with a loo and a washbasin, and a sort of open bit where the boat gets narrow at the front, full of ropes and anchors and stuff."

"What were the berths like? What color were they?"

"I seem to remember they were covered in some green material. Dark green, I think—but I'm not sure. It's a long time ago—and I wasn't paying any special attention. I mean, why should I? *I* didn't know anyone would want me to give a description of the boat."

"Fair enough," I said. "Right—so you had drinks. . . . What did you drink, by the way?"

"Oh, *really!* Probably gin-and-tonic—and I think Jim had whisky. But I wouldn't swear to it."

"And after the drinks—what?"

14

"Well, we were having a wonderful time, and it was beginning to get dark, and the evening was so lovely and peaceful out there on the water, and presently Jim said what a pity it was I had to go back. I said I did have to, because I had to catch the morning boat to Oban on account of my new job, and he said he could easily drop me near the town in the early morning and I could still catch the boat. So, to cut a long story short, I stayed."

"And what happened?"

Shirley looked me straight in the eye. "What do you think happened?"

"You mean he seduced you?"

"Good gracious, no, he didn't have to. We just made love, and it was beautiful. After all, why not? He was free and I was free and we liked each other and we both wanted to. I don't blame him in the least for what happened and I don't see why he should feel guilty about it. We were just being natural."

"And then?"

"Well, I slept marvelously—Jim had got a spare sleeping bag which was very cozy—and he woke me with a cup of tea just before it got light, and then he took me in the rubber boat to near Tobermory and I walked the last bit along the cliff path to the motel. I rumpled the bedclothes in my room and packed my things and had breakfast, and then I caught the steamer to Oban and went straight on to London."

"Had you made any arrangement with Jim to meet again?"

"No—there didn't seem much point, when I was going abroad for the whole winter anyway—though it wasn't just that. Jim didn't volunteer his address or phone number or anything and I thought probably he didn't want to continue the thing, and I quite understood. It was a sort of amorous adventure, a beautiful holiday memory, and I didn't want him to think I was trying to tie him down to anything. So we said goodbye, and thanks for everything, and that was that."

"But you did try to get in touch with him again when you got back."

"That was just an impulse—I hadn't really intended to. But I saw this piece in the paper about his meeting—that was when I discovered he was an M.P.; there wasn't anything else about him in the bit I read—and his picture was there, which brought everything back, and I thought it would be nice to see him again if he felt like it and wasn't too busy, so I went along, thinking I could speak to him afterward, and when I couldn't get in I sent him a note. It was just a friendly move—it was entirely up to him what he did. If he merely hadn't replied to the note, I wouldn't have been too surprised. . . . But what he's done now—telling everyone he never knew me—I think that's really mean. It puts me in a terrible position."

By now I was beginning to think that this could be one of the stories of the century—not so much because of what Lester was supposed to have done as because he'd denied it. The girl's account had seemed to me pretty convincing. I didn't see how we could use much of it—not at the moment, anyway—but it seemed worthwhile to make a play for exclusive rights in case things developed. So I said, "You know, Miss Holt, if you were prepared to give my paper the sole rights to your story" —and I explained in detail what I meant, because she obviously hadn't a clue—"I think it might be worth quite a lot to you. Perhaps as much as a thousand pounds—perhaps more. Of course, I'd have to speak to my editor before I could make a definite offer, but I could do that right away on the telephone."

She turned me down with indignation. "I wouldn't think of taking money," she said. "You surely don't imagine I'm on the make. I've only told you all this because—well, because I felt I'd been horribly let down, and I just had to tell somebody. I wouldn't dream of taking a penny."

I said I'd been sure all the time that she wouldn't, but my paper would expect me to have asked—and I handed her her shopping bag and said I hoped we'd meet again sometime.

It will be appreciated that I took no notes during our talk, for fear of scaring her off. I have tried to reconstruct our conversation as faithfully as possible from memory. The quotes are not to be taken literally, but the gist of our exchanges is right, and I have tried to convey the atmosphere.

My own feeling, for what it is worth, is that Shirley Holt is a nice, intelligent, rather unconventional girl of considerable personality, who understandably resents being called a liar in public and is probably telling the truth.

5

SOURCE. Linda Tandy's diary. Monday, April 16th.

What an absolutely frightful day! That girl seems to have talked to every reporter in London—including our Fred Savory, so at least we're up to date—and her expanded version of what happened on and around that Scottish beach is quite hair-raising in its possible consequences for James. Fleet Street is seething with excitement and frustration. No British paper can print the whole thing for fear of libel, but some of them are planning carefully edited stories which they hope will get past their lawyers. It'll all come out before long anyway—the word is that the New York *Echo* man saw Shirley Holt this afternoon, and of course they don't have to worry about libel; they'll publish every last word, and so will the Continentals, and then there'll be no holding anyone.

James repeated to Noll this morning that he'd never met the girl—but that was before she came out with all the corroborative detail about himself and the boat. I want so much to believe she's made the whole story up, but it isn't easy in the face of the evidence. One has to be realistic. Why *shouldn't* James have done what she says? What would be so surprising? He's a normal man, and she's very attractive, damn her, and he has no ties, and he must have felt very lonely and deprived since Mary. Common sense suggests that she's telling the truth.

And yet—and yet . . . Perhaps I'm being simple, but to me James doesn't fit the role. The story as it stands makes him out a light man, a *lightweight* man, a casual man, an unfastidious man—and the James I know is none of these things; in fact, he's exactly the opposite. Also, I find it hard to believe that if he had met the girl as she says, he'd have denied it *personally* to Noll, his oldest and closest friend.

But I could be so wrong. . . .

It's all rather hell—I wish I didn't have such vivid mental pictures. I'm trying to put that side of it out of my mind, but it's not easy.

Midnight

E. rang me this afternoon, for about the fourth time in a month, and asked if by any chance I was free for dinner and a show, because he'd got two stalls for *Spider's Web*. I said yes, in a kind of rage with James, which was most unfair. E. is one of the F.O.'s oncoming young men— very good company, actually, as well as being very presentable—and it should have been fun, but I just couldn't get in the mood. After the show he suggested the usual "one for the road" at his flat and I said all right, feeling a bit conscience-stricken, and of course he made a pass but I couldn't respond. He said all I needed was "awakening," which was so unbelievably corny I just had to laugh. I said I'd already been "awakened," several times, but the trouble was I could never *keep* awake. He gave up in the end and played two sides of Berlioz and then drove me home.

I had another word with Noll before bed. He wouldn't commit himself to a positive view on the story, but he's obviously worried stiff by the girl's latest statements and James's continued denials. He says that, politically, we're sitting on a bomb that could blow us sky-high in a week. He thinks it possible that James, having made his initial spur-of-the-moment disclaimer, may now feel stuck with it, and unable to get himself off the hook. He tried to make contact tonight, but James was caught up in the election whirl and wasn't available. So he's sent a note round instead.

18

6

SOURCE. Note from Oliver Tandy to James Lester. Marked "Urgent and Personal." Monday, April 16th.

(Oliver Tandy is 52. He has spent his whole adult life in journalism, starting as a reporter on the old *News Chronicle*. Edited the London *Review* for five years, resigned over a question of policy. Has edited the *Post* with marked success for nine years. An outstanding figure in Fleet Street, widely respected and admired. A man of strong views: independent, resourceful, and courageous. *Ed.*)

Fleet Street
6 P.M.

My dear Jim,

I've been trying hard to get hold of you but couldn't catch up with your rapid movements. So I'm sending this note by hand to your HQ in the hope that it will reach you by nightfall.

I imagine you'll have heard by now what Shirley Holt has been telling the world. In case you haven't had the full picture, I enclose a transcript of our man's report.

The thing that's bothering a lot of people, not least your friends, is the very circumstantial description she gives of the boat, and the detailed knowledge she obviously has of you personally.

Jim, I've known you so long and so well that I claim the right to speak frankly. A situation is building up which could destroy you. If you still say that the girl is lying, I shall of course believe you, and you may count on my wholehearted support and help whatever the consequences that may follow. But if you *were* with her that day, for God's sake come clean now. It's not too late. You could say you denied it at first because you were concerned for the girl's reputation—a consideration that no longer applies, since she's told the story herself. People would understand that. And who could criticize you, a free man, for having an affair with an unmarried girl? It happens quite often, after all! They'd say it was only human. It might even help you.

You may think this note impertinent or intrusive—though I hope not. If I seem to be talking out of turn, you must forgive me. "For 'tis my love that speaks."

Yours ever,
Noll

7

SOURCE. Note from James Lester to Oliver Tandy. Monday, April 16th.

Progressive Party HQ
Smith Square, S.W. 1.
11:30 P.M.

Dear Noll,

Many thanks for your note. I've been kept pretty well up to date with today's developments by my press secretary, but your reporter fills in some details which I'm glad to have. Far from thinking your remarks impertinent or intrusive, I was moved by your affectionate concern. If one can't speak one's mind after twenty years of friendship, what's friendship for?

20

I've been reflecting on what you said about the likely reaction of people if I "came clean." For once, I can't agree with you. I know we live in a permissive age, but I doubt if the permissiveness extends to prospective Prime Ministers who pick up strange girls on beaches, lie around with them nude at an hour's acquaintance, sleep with them for a night, and then think no more about it. Where their leaders are concerned, the masses are puritan—they expect standards of personal behavior whiter than white. And I think they're right. Nobody *has* to put himself forward as a leader, a molder of thought and opinion—whether as a politician, a clergyman, a headmaster, or a judge. If he does, he must be like Caesar's wife. It's part of an unwritten contract, which he breaks at his peril. If I now admitted what Miss Holt alleges, I'm quite certain I would have no chance of leading my party to victory, and I think I would deserve defeat.

However, these rather pompous thoughts have no relevance to my situation. Miss Holt *is* lying, and no one would expect me to admit something that I didn't do. So I welcome the trust you offer me (I hope it's shared by Linda), and I expect to be taking you up on your promise of support and help, which clearly I am going to need.

I talked the whole matter over this evening with Geoffrey Blossom. He shares your political anxieties, as of course I do myself. As you know, he didn't favor me as leader when Grantley died, but his loyalty to the party is absolute and as Chief Whip his main concern is naturally for the party. I thought he put the situation very succinctly, if not very flatteringly. He said, "If the girl's story is untrue but you can't convince enough people, we shall lose the election. If the girl's story is true and you're forced by mounting evidence to admit it later, there'll be a landslide against us, because the voters never forgive public lying."

I repeated that I knew nothing of the girl (I *think* he believed me), and on that basis we went on to discuss possible courses of action. One was to issue a writ for slander and try to get an injunction, but we agreed that with an election pending this would be seen by many as an attempt to stifle discussion till after polling day, and politically would do more harm than good. We also agreed that at present there were no grounds for police investigation or action. The alternative, disagreeable though it seemed, was to bring the whole thing out into the open and fight it through. This is what we've decided to do. I shall be holding a special press conference here tomorrow, when I shall make a statement and answer questions. After it's over, perhaps you and Linda and I can meet to discuss battle plans.

I hope this reaches you tonight. Hailey passes your flat on his way home, and has promised to drop it in.

Sleep well, old friend. The truth will prevail.

Yours ever,
Jim

8

SOURCE. Report in the *Times* of James Lester's press conference held at Progressive Party HQ, Smith Square, on the morning of Tuesday, April 17th.

(The conference was attended by some 100 newsmen from the U.K. and world press, and TV and radio networks. Lester was flanked by Geoffrey Blossom, the party Chief Whip, and Eric Craven, the chairman of the parliamentary party. In a few introductory words, Mr. Craven indicated that the proceedings would be informal and that reporters should remain seated when asking questions. Lester then took charge of the conference. He made the following opening statement, and subsequently answered questions for an hour. *Ed.*)

As I am sure you all know, ladies and gentlemen, it has been alleged by a Miss Shirley Holt that I met her last September on a Scottish beach when I was holidaying in my boat, that I swam and sunbathed naked with her, that I later made love to her on the boat, where she spent the night, and that I put her ashore early next morning near Tobermory. You will recall that I denied all knowledge of her when the matter was first raised at one of my meetings. I have since seen many photographs of her. I now repeat that I never in my life met Miss Holt, and that all her allegations are totally untrue. I have this morning sworn an affidavit to that effect, and copies of the document will be made available to you. You will see, therefore, that I am staking not only my reputation and my political career but also my personal freedom on the truth of what I am saying.

My colleagues and I have naturally considered the advisability of issuing a writ for slander and seeking a temporary injunction. This might gag Miss Holt for the time being, but it would hardly allay public disquiet. Indeed, it might well increase it, since the feeling would be that I was trying to hush things up till the election was over, which is the very opposite of my intention. The truth in this unsavory affair can best be served by bringing everything out into the light of day, and I propose to do all I can to assist the process. I am not, of course, ruling out the possibility of legal action against Miss Holt at a later date.

In view of my position as leader of Her Majesty's Opposition, and in view of the election campaign now just beginning, I accept that Miss Holt's allegations are a matter of great and legitimate public interest and concern, and as such should be open to free public discussion and comment in speech and in the press and on other media without fear of legal consequences. I therefore give this guarantee: that I shall take no legal action at any time against the media or against any individual on account of anything they may write or say in good faith about this affair. You have a free hand, ladies and gentlemen—to report, to investigate, to comment, to criticize, or to crucify.

Before I invite your questions, I think it would be helpful if I gave you my own account of what took place at the time the allegations refer to.

I had arranged to have a holiday on my boat, cruising the Western Isles of Scotland, with Mr. Oliver Tandy, the Editor of the *Post*, as my companion. We traveled together on August 25th to Oban, where the boat had been left since Whitsun, and for a week or more we cruised as planned. Then, on September 3rd, when we were in port at Tobermory, a message reached Mr. Tandy saying that his father was dangerously ill, and he had to return to London. I continued to sail for a day or two, single-handed, in an unambitious way, making short trips from Tobermory and returning there each night.

On September 5th, which is the day Miss Holt's allegations refer to, I took on fuel and small stores preparatory to sailing that evening through the Sound of Mull to Oban, where I again planned to leave the boat. In the early afternoon, I left harbor and anchored offshore some three miles north of Tobermory to await a favorable tide. I spent the next few hours reading and resting in the cabin, so that I would be fresh for the night passage. Around dusk I weighed anchor and set off for Oban. The weather, which had been very fine, was showing signs of becoming less settled, and with a head wind I decided to use the engine. All went well until just before midnight, when a piece of flotsam got caught in the propeller. I tried to free it by reversing the engine, but had no success. I limped into shallow water and anchored, and tried using the boat hook, first from the cockpit and then from the dinghy, but again without success. So I hoisted the sails and continued on my way, tacking up through the Sound. But because of the delay I was soon faced with an adverse tide, and made slow progress. The wind was rising —nothing dramatic, but a fresh breeze—and I was a little concerned about being blown hard aground on a tack. Sometime before dawn, I decided it would be wiser to turn back to Tobermory and try again when conditions were better. I had a very fast run back with favorable wind and tide, got into harbor just before first light, and tied up. That afternoon, I went through the Sound under engine without trouble, left the boat at Oban in charge of a yard, and returned by train to London that night.

Now let's have your questions.

Q: You say, sir, that you spent the afternoon of September 5th anchored offshore about three miles north of Tobermory. Would that not have put you roughly in the position where Miss Holt says she saw you?

A: Roughly, I would think, yes.

Q: How far offshore were you anchored?

A: About three hundred yards.

Q: Did you go ashore at any time during that afternoon or evening?

A: No.

Q: Did you notice anyone on the beach at any time?

A: No. As I say, I was resting in the cabin. I didn't inspect the shore closely.

Q: Did you have any special reason for going to an offshore anchorage, instead of waiting for your tide in harbor?

A: Yes. Harbors are noisy places. I wanted to be quiet.

Q: Did you come across any other boat or ship on your night passage —anyone who might remember seeing you?

A: I don't know about remembering me. The only boat that came near me wasn't paying proper attention and almost ran me down. It was a very large motor cruiser, with blazing cabin and deck lights and a radio blaring. It was traveling in the opposite direction, toward Tobermory, and going very fast—about fifteen knots, I'd guess. It sheered away in the nick of time.

Q: About what time would that have been?

A: I would think about eleven o'clock.

Q: When you were still under engine?

A: Yes.

Q: Then couldn't you have taken avoiding action?

A *(smile):* I tried to. There are limits to what you can do with six knots against fifteen, especially when the other fellow is steering an erratic course.

25

Q: Did you get the name of this cruiser, sir?

A: Unfortunately not. I couldn't make out the name because of the bright lights aboard. They were quite dazzling.

Q: Was it a British boat?

A: I rather doubt it. Someone shouted at me as it went past, and the words didn't sound English.

Q: Could they have been Scottish? *(Laughter)*

Q: Did this boat have a flag? If so, surely it would have shown up in the lights?

A: It was flying something at the stern, but the flag was drooping round the pole so I couldn't make out what it was.

Q: What made you set out for Oban at night, instead of in the daytime?

A: It made a change—and I rather enjoy night passages. I'm not unique in that—many yachtsmen do. The weather's often quieter, and the shore and buoy lights make navigation easier.

Q: If in fact, sir, you *didn't* attempt this passage but were anchored offshore with Miss Holt aboard—I put it as a pure hypothesis, of course—wouldn't you naturally say you undertook the passage at night, when not being seen by anyone would be understandable?

A *(grim smile):* Your reasoning is sound, but your pure hypothesis is not.

Q: Miss Holt says you put her ashore just before it got light. You say you re-entered Tobermory harbor just before it got light. Have you any comment to make on that coincidence?

A: No comment at all.

Q: As it wasn't light when you re-entered harbor, presumably nobody saw you come in?

A: I don't know whether anyone saw me or not. I imagine most people would have been asleep.

Q: Did you discover what had jammed your propeller?

A: Yes, a piece of rope. I poked it out from the quayside with the boat hook later that morning.

Q: Did anyone see you do that?

A: I've no idea.

Q: Sir, I've been going over my notes of Miss Holt's story as she told it to me in an interview, and I find that she mentioned no fewer than twenty-two items of purportedly factual information concerning your boat, and nine more items concerning yourself, several of them of a rather personal nature. I imagine that by now you may have seen a similar list of items yourself?

A: Yes, I have.

Q: Have you discovered any inaccuracies in the list?

A: No. I haven't had time yet to consider every item in detail, but my initial impression is that all the descriptive and personal information she gave is correct.

Q: Miss Holt says, of course, that all the information came from you, or from her own observation at the time, when she was aboard the boat. Can you suggest how otherwise she could have acquired so much detailed knowledge?

A: That's something I shall be giving a good deal of thought to. I've a few ideas about it, but at the moment I prefer not to speculate.

Q: She said that you were wearing yellow slacks and canvas shoes on the beach that day. Were you?

A: If that's meant as a trap, Mr.—er—Blakey, isn't it?—I take a dim view of it. As far as the slacks and shoes in general are concerned, that was often my wear on board—and it was my wear on board that day.

Q: Without a shirt?

A: Probably. It was a hot day.

Q: Miss Holt has said she couldn't remember the name of your boat. What is its name?

A: It was called *Raradoa*. It had that name when I bought it, and I didn't bother to change it.

Q: In view of its name, would you consider Miss Holt's failure to remember it reasonable?

A: If the rest of her story had been true, yes.

Q: If she *had* remembered it, wouldn't you have been rather surprised?

A: I don't think anything that Miss Holt remembered would surprise me. *(Laughter)*

Q: I believe, sir, you sold your boat during the winter. Many of us would be glad of an opportunity to check some of the descriptions ourselves. Could you give us the name of the new owner?

A: I'd prefer not to mention any names at all at this session—but the boat is registered, so you'll have no trouble in getting the information you want.

Q: Did you have any special reason for selling the boat?

A: Only that I didn't think I'd have much time to use it. I had it brought down to the East Coast after I was elected to the Shadow Cabinet, thinking it might be handy for the odd weekend. Then I realized I'd be too busy, anyway, and got rid of it. A boat you don't use is a very expensive luxury.

Q: Reverting to Miss Holt, sir, could you suggest any *reason* why she should have made what you say are totally false allegations?

A: No. Naturally I've been thinking about that a great deal, but at the moment I've no explanation to offer.

Q: Would you be willing to confront her publicly?

A: I can't imagine that any useful purpose would be served by that. I assume Miss Holt would merely repeat her charges, and I should continue to deny them, and probably I should get very angry. It would no doubt be good TV spectacle—but I don't relish the idea of being butchered to make a TV holiday.

Q: What action are you going to take over all this, sir?

A: Well, my friends and I will be making all sorts of inquiries. I don't think this is the time to go into details. Naturally you'll be kept informed about developments.

Q: Is this affair going to affect your campaign schedule?

A: I hope not—though it's hard to know at this stage how much time it's going to take up. My present intention is to continue to campaign as though it hadn't happened. I need hardly say that I consider it a most regrettable and basically trivial development, and I wish it hadn't been necessary to take it seriously.

Q: How do you think it's going to affect your election chances?

A *(a wry smile):* I'm not a prophet. You tell me!

9

SOURCE. Linda Tandy's diary. Tuesday, April 17th.

I've just read the transcript of James's press conference—with rather mixed feelings.

In one way, of course, I'm enormously relieved, because it's as clear to me now as anything could be that he *didn't* meet Shirley Holt and that on that score I've been worrying for nothing. No one could have been more patently honest and open than he was, with his straightforward account of his night trip and his refusal to theorize where he hadn't any knowledge. Swearing that affidavit must have made a great impression on everyone, too, for no one lightly courts a three-year sentence for perjury. In his quiet way, James has quite a sense of drama—though I suppose all top politicians have something of the actor about them. Noll says he handled the press conference beautifully, and the transcript bears that out. It can't be easy to keep your dignity and your good humor when you're being grilled publicly on intimate personal matters and virtually being called a liar half the time.

What appalls me is that all this should have had to happen to James. It's really monstrous that a man of his integrity should be put virtually on trial over something he didn't do and knows nothing about, and have to answer a lot of barbed questions about his actions and behavior. How he must have loathed it! But it's hard to see how he could have avoided it in the circumstances. If the girl could have been brought *quickly* to court, that would have been another matter—but there was never a chance of that.

Of course, we're still sitting on the bomb—and denials and statements alone won't defuse it. What we need now is supporting evidence for James, or an effective counterattack, or both. James is snatching some time off to come to the office this afternoon for a discussion of the whole problem.

What *can* that girl be up to?

Later

James arrived just after three o'clock. He looked a little tired, which wasn't surprising after his grueling morning, but he didn't seem nearly as upset by what had happened as I'd have expected—not outwardly, anyway. I said I didn't know how he managed to keep so calm when *I* was positively seething, and he said with a grin that a man who panicked over a minor personal difficulty would hardly make much of a Prime Minister!

Anyway, now to our council of war.

As a preliminary, we studied, practically word by word, the message that Shirley Holt had sent to James at his adoption meeting, which he'd brought along with him. We were hoping, of course, for some slipup, some false note that didn't accord with what she'd said later. In the main, it seemed just the sort of message she would have sent if her story had been true. "Remember me?—Shirley Holt." Fair enough, after one night with a man and a seven-month gap. "I got back from my travels yesterday"—well, she'd said she'd mentioned her plans. "I expect you're rather busy"—that would follow from her having discovered, as she'd said, that James was an M.P. "I'm still at Egerton Road. . . ."

That was more interesting. Shirley hadn't said she'd given James her

30

address, but it was implicit in the note. Why would she have done that if—as she'd stated—she'd thought he probably didn't want to continue the affair? There seemed a small discrepancy here. And *when* would she have done it? Not, surely, early in their supposed talk. She might have said, "I live in Surbiton," but she'd hardly have said at that stage, "I live in Egerton Road, Surbiton." You usually only give your full address to a new acquaintance on parting. That thought raised another query in my mind. James, she'd indicated, hadn't volunteered his own address. That seemed to me a rather extraordinary situation. If you meet a man, and spend a cozy night with him, and give him your address in the morning, surely he has to reciprocate in some way—even if he only gives a false address, or something vague like c/o his bank. To make no response at all would be pretty insulting, yet Shirley appeared to have accepted it without a murmur. It seemed another unexplained point in her story, and I suggested that one of our sleuths should do a bit more probing, and the others agreed.

We moved on then to discuss the first of the really basic questions —how Shirley could have known so much—starting with the things James was supposed to have told her about himself, like having once been a barrister, and about Mary's death in an accident, and so on. James thought there was no insuperable difficulty there, because several "profiles" of him had appeared in the press in recent weeks, giving these and a lot of other personal details, and Shirley could have been a more diligent reader of newspapers than she pretended. Just how she'd found out about James's sailing companion being called away was more puzzling, though Noll thought there might have been a brief mention of the recall in some paper, in connection with Grandfather's death. Or, of course, she could have got her information from someone else.

Then there was the matter of her boat description. It had seemed a big hurdle, and a worrying one, but James was rather reassuring. He said that after going through her statement again item by item he'd come to the conclusion that she hadn't mentioned anything so far that she couldn't have seen by walking round the quay at Tobermory and looking through the open cabin door when he was aboard, or through the windows. The quay was a favorite place for holiday strolling and gaping because of all the port activity, and there were seats under the wall in the sun where people sometimes sat for hours, watching what was going on and studying the boats. Noll agreed about that. Alternatively, James said, the girl might have seen the boat at some other time and place—after it was sold, for instance—though not, of course, if she'd been abroad all winter as she claimed. A third possibility was that, again, she'd got the information from someone else. That opened a huge field of choice. There were dozens of people who could have given the sort of description of the boat that she'd given. In Tobermory alone there'd been too many to count—fellow yachtsmen James had chatted with on the quay or had aboard for a drink; people who'd taken his ropes or helped to cast off; the man who'd filled his fuel tank; the man who'd brought groceries aboard; the harbor master who'd fixed him up with his berth—not to mention casual observers. Then there was all the yard staff at Oban, where the boat had been left, and the new owner, and all the people the new owner must have shown the boat to. In fact, the list was endless.

Clearly, we were nowhere near discovering *how* Shirley had got her knowledge. But we'd gone some way toward showing that she hadn't necessarily got it through James.

Next we came to the question of how Shirley could have learned so much about James's plans and movements while he was at Tobermory on his own. It was Noll who raised this. He pointed out that unless the girl was a half-wit, which she showed no sign of being, she wouldn't have dared to make her allegation unless she'd *known* that James had been at sea all night with no alibi; otherwise he might have come up with some incontrovertible proof that he'd been somewhere else, and she'd have been done for. A very important point, we agreed. All we could think of, again, was (1) that she'd been lazing about on the quay and perhaps overheard James talking about his plans and/or his abortive trip to fellow yachtsmen or the harbor master or someone, or (2) that she'd got the information from someone else. Once more, the choice was too wide to be of any help. James said he'd probably mentioned the trip in a casual way to at least half a dozen people at Tobermory, before and after he'd undertaken it, and he'd no doubt told many people since, including yachting colleagues at the House, because the slight mishap with the engine and his efforts to put it right made a good sailing yarn among people who were interested. Apart from that, he seemed to remember there'd been a gossip paragraph about it in some paper at the time—or maybe in a yachting journal—so virtually anybody could have known.

We considered briefly the related point of how Shirley could have known that James's boat had been anchored offshore that afternoon, and where. There was less difficulty here. It was quite possible that she had been on the beach herself, or perhaps strolling on the cliff-top path, and if she'd already seen the boat with its red sails in harbor, she would have recognized it. Incidentally, I pointed out, if she'd been watching the boat coming in to anchor, that might have been the moment when she'd noted the bare torso, yellow slacks, and canvas shoes that she'd mentioned in her story.

The next question we discussed was what possible motive Shirley could have for making her allegations. Noll said it didn't appear to be money, since she'd indignantly turned down the possibility of a thousand pounds or more from the *News*. James wondered if she might be holding out for a bigger offer from someone later, but Noll said he very much doubted it, as in that case she would hardly have gone on pouring out the stuff for free to all comers. We agreed that if she'd made some sort of discreet approach to James, one could have suspected a blackmail attempt, but she'd done the opposite. In short, there didn't seem to be any prospect of financial advantage for her out of this aspect of the affair at all.

We turned to the political angle. Was she trying to destroy James and/or his party because of what they stood for? The fact that she appeared to be a political illiterate didn't necessarily mean anything.

33

After all, we *knew* she was putting on a big act, and a very persuasive one, so she was obviously good at dissimulation. Could she be a crypto-something? Noll said he just couldn't imagine anyone thinking the game worth the candle, politically, because James and his party were essentially moderates, and it was usually only fanatical extremists who provoked extreme action. If James and the Progressives won the election, there'd be no dramatic or disruptive changes, merely a livelier administration—so why go to such lengths to destroy them? He couldn't see that anyone stood to gain anything politically from the allegations.

As far as policy was concerned, I agreed with him. Destroying James wouldn't change the national scene all that much. But it might, I pointed out, change the scene quite a bit for certain individuals. James's election as party leader had been a close-run thing, and there'd been some bitter infighting beforehand. As I recalled, he'd collected 132 votes on the first ballot, with the elderly but still ambitious Leslie Shirman runner-up with 124 votes, and Dudley French, young and brash but very able, only a little behind with 108. If James were now to disappear from the picture, one of those two could well become Prime Minister. Which, theoretically, was quite a motive for action. However, in the total absence of evidence, the notion that one of them might have connived with Shirley Holt to ruin James seemed altogether too farfetched to be seriously entertained, and we didn't pursue it.

So we came to the third possible explanation. Was the girl some sort of a nut case? Was she like those women who make baseless accusations of attempted rape against strange men? It was a little hard to believe. For one thing, she was the wrong age, and also there was too much thought and method and too little impulse in her accusations. She certainly hadn't shown any outward and obvious signs of disturbance—and there wasn't much hope of probing deeper, since she wasn't in the least likely to agree to a psychiatric examination. But she *could* be a case, of some sort. Was she, Noll wondered, one of those people who have a compulsion to achieve notoriety, whatever the cost? It rather went with her lack of reticence in talking so freely to the press, and she'd certainly hit the world headlines—though of course, he added, once the story had broken she'd have had to go into a nunnery if she'd wanted to escape reporters.

On the whole, we rather went for some sort of psychological motive, as the best bet of the three.

Then Noll raised a further point. There was an aspect that bothered him, he said, about both the political and the notoriety motives. It seemed to him that there were two possibilities:

1. That Shirley (or someone) had collected and made notes of essential items of information while she (or someone) was at Tobermory. But at that time James was a comparative unknown. No one could have guessed he was going to become a worthwhile political target, or that an accusation against him would bring great notoriety. As far as the James of that period was concerned, the sort of allegation Shirley had made, even if proved true, would have been of only passing interest outside his own constituency.

2. That Shirley saw some political or notoriety attraction only after James had become the prospective top man—i.e., a few weeks ago. But that would mean that after more than six months she'd have had to recollect in detail (or someone would) facts and events which at the time could have been of no more than minor interest to a holidaymaker, or to most people.

We mulled over it for a while, but we none of us had any answer to the puzzle. So we left it.

We turned next to the urgent practical question—what we were going to *do*. Noll took the lead in this. For one thing, he'd had time to think about it and draw up a sort of mental list. And, of course, he had the reporters to do the work. I can't think how James would have managed without him, because no private inquiry agency could begin to cope with the crash program that's needed in the short time before the election. Whereas we can deploy a dozen men if necessary—all as good as any private eye. And as they're mostly sold on the Progressive

Party anyway (reporters usually tend to gravitate to papers of their own political leanings), they'll be keen.

Our discussion on what to do started with a bit of an argy-bargy. Obviously, Noll said, our greatest need was for unbiased testimony supporting James's account of what had happened on September 5th, and he suggested we should go all out to get independent confirmation that James had intended to make the passage to Oban that night and had told people so at the time. James—precise and logical, as usual—pointed out that whether or not he had *intended* to go didn't really affect the issue; he might well have gone out to the anchorage with the intention, seen the girl on the beach, made contact with her, and subsequently changed his mind. Noll saw the force of that and switched his ground. Perhaps, he said, we could find witnesses to say that James had told them about the abortive passage *afterward.* That surely would help? The snag there, James thought—looking at it from the point of view of a critical outsider—was that as he'd told people about his projected trip beforehand, he'd naturally have had to give some explanation of why he was back in Tobermory in the morning. And since he wouldn't have wanted to say he'd spent the night offshore with a girl, the simplest thing would have been to say he'd attempted the passage and failed. Noll said that might apply to an explanation given at the time, but what about the account he'd given afterward, when he was back in London—to Noll himself, for instance? Didn't that prove something? James replied that once having committed himself to an explanation, it would have seemed safer to stick to it. I said, but would he have gone into all that corroborative detail about the motor cruiser—with Noll, back in London—if it hadn't been true? Wouldn't he just have stuck to the simple explanation without trimmings? And it then turned out, rather disconcertingly, that he hadn't mentioned the cruiser to Noll. He'd been reminded of it, he said, only as a result of the question at the press conference.

Anyway, after all this chat we finally agreed that on balance the production of witnesses who would say that James had mentioned his intention and described his attempted passage to them after his return would be decidedly more helpful than not. It would be something to give to the press, and was definitely worth trying for. Our jury, after all, was to be the nation, not a group of logicians. The question was, who were these hoped-for witnesses, and how and where were we going to find them?

At first, the only person James could suggest—apart from Noll himself, who was known to be such a close friend that his evidence might be discounted—was the harbor master at Tobermory. That seemed a pretty good start to me, but Noll wanted more and pressed James about other yachtsmen he'd talked to: couldn't he remember any names at all, or the names of any of their boats? James considered, and said he didn't think so—it really was a case of ships that pass in the night; you had a chat and maybe a drink but, unless there was some special reason, you didn't exchange names, or if you exchanged them you didn't remember them. For instance, there'd been a couple of men he'd certainly told about his plans, because they'd just come through the Sound themselves, and the three of them had talked about it—but he'd never got their names. They were a pair of wide boys from the south, James said, both around thirty, who'd described themselves as "directors." Apparently they'd shared a fairly big pools win and they'd come up to Oban and hired a 20-foot speedboat with a shiny hard top like a car and lots of chromium and two enormous Evinrude outboards. "They were really water motorists," James said. "When I told them I planned to go through the Sound, one of them said, 'There's nothing to it, mate—it's a piece o' cake. We did it in one hour twelve minutes flat'—which meant they'd averaged about twenty-two knots!"

Noll grinned. "Keep going, Jim. What else do you know about them?"

"Nothing else," James said. "Except that they were heavy drinkers—particularly one of them. They'd had a case of champagne delivered aboard to celebrate their luck, and each night this chap got tight on it. So tight, once, that he went overboard. They were tied up to the quay at around half tide, with very loose ropes, and they were using a ladder to climb ashore, propped up against the slippery wall, and this fellow started up the ladder sometime after dark, with a lot of noise that brought me out of my cabin, and as he climbed the ladder he naturally pushed the boat away from the quayside and the ladder began to go down and the chap yelled, 'Christ, I'm going in!' And he did go in, between the boat and the quay, and I had to help fish him out. . . . But I never learned who they were."

"If they hired a speedboat in Oban, we may be able to trace them," Noll said. "Now, who else did you talk to?"

James pondered. "Well, there was another man berthed quite near me who'd been collecting a boat from one of the islands. An interesting fellow—a professional yacht-deliverer. I had some long chats with him and I certainly told him my plans—but I'm blessed if I remember his name—" James broke off. "Wait a minute, perhaps I do have his name. . . ." He took out his wallet and poked around in it. "Yes—here we are." He produced a card and showed us. It read, "Frank Jackson, Yacht Deliverer, West Mersea, Essex," and gave a telephone number. "I asked him for his card," James said, "because I thought I might need his services some time."

"You were right," Noll said, "you *do* need his services. Let's hope he's not in the South Seas."

So there we were, with our first bits of action lined up. Someone would go to Tobermory and interview the harbor master; someone else would try to trace the two boat hirers; and a third man would go to West Mersea and interview Jackson. And if they all confirmed that James had mentioned his plans and described his attempted passage to them, that would at least be something for our public jury to chew over. If it did nothing else, it would show that we were fighting back.

We hadn't lost sight, during all this talk, of the importance of the motor cruiser that had nearly run James down. If we could identify that, and find someone who remembered the incident, we'd be well on our way. But it clearly wasn't going to be easy, since we didn't know the vessel's name or nationality or where it had come from or where it was bound for or even what it looked like; and in view of the publicity James had given to its bad seamanship, whoever had been in charge might well be reluctant to come forward. However, we certainly had to try. Our best hope, we decided, was to advertise in a wide variety of newspapers: the Scottish ones, of course; the leading English ones, which a foreign yacht owner might possibly see; and the main papers in all the major countries whose citizens were free to own yachts. The advertisement would also go into a selection of yachting magazines, though as these were mostly monthlies it probably wouldn't appear there for quite a while. James drew up a tactful draft, which Noll and I approved after some minor changes. It ran:

This is an SOS to all international yachtsmen. Will the owner of a large motor cruiser, bound nor'westward through the Sound of Mull toward Tobermory, Isle of Mull, Scotland, at about 2300 hours British time on September 5th last, and which changed course to avoid a small yacht traveling in the opposite direction under power and now thought to have been inadequately lit, please communicate with James Lester, M.P., House of Commons, Westminster, London? The reward will be the knowledge of an inestimable service to a fellow yachtsman.

We were quite pleased with that, and Noll sent it down to the Foreign Room to be translated into all the necessary languages before being passed on to Graham, our Advertising Manager, for action.

Our discussion of steps to be taken came finally to Shirley Holt herself. Obviously there was going to be a lot of work to be done on her. First, there were her movements on Mull. After a gap of seven months the trail would be pretty cold, but if by some lucky chance anyone could be found who could say that he'd seen her at her motel during the vital evening or night, she'd be dished. It was a long shot, but worth the effort, and the reporter who interviewed the harbor master could take that in as well. Then someone should certainly talk to the agency Shirley had said she'd used, and we ought to try and get from Shirley herself all possible details of the people she'd worked for since Mull, and of her movements abroad. We should also need to go into her general background and record in the greatest possible detail.

As we were finishing with Shirley, James came up with a point so obvious that I couldn't imagine how we hadn't thought of it before. If she'd really spent a night aboard the boat, he said, her description wouldn't have been confined to things she could have seen from the quay; she'd have remembered all sorts of details from inside. So when she was next interviewed, she should be pressed for a more precise description. If she couldn't produce anything new, that would be most significant, and would certainly help to reduce her credibility.

So there we are, with a terrific program of work ahead. But at least James is being relieved of some of his burden, and can try to concentrate on his rallies and conferences and TV interviews and baby-kissing—if he does kiss babies. I somehow doubt it.

Later still

After James had gone, Noll and I discussed briefly which reporter could best do what job. Normally, of course, it's the News Editor, John Thresher, who decides who should go on assignments—sometimes after consultation with Noll, but more often not. I certainly wouldn't have anything to do with it. But this was a special situation, and I did know all the reporters very well, having nattered with them for years over indifferent meals in the office canteen.

As it happened, Noll's views and mine pretty well coincided.

For seeing the harbor master and nosing around in Tobermory, we thought George Bromley. He's a big, bulky man of about fifty, good with officials and policemen (the boys say he looks like a worn-out cop himself), and he likes to be on the move to get away from his Hungarian wife—"my bloody wife," he calls her. He gets baited over that quite a bit, and also about his "system." Whenever he has a few moments free in the reporters' room, he takes a sheaf of lined papers from his drawer and six bottles of different-colored inks and gets to work on what's reputed to be a highly profitable racing system. Personally, I think he just knows a lot about horses. He's an eccentric character, but very plodding and reliable on a job.

For chasing up the two boat hirers, and then holding himself in readiness for anything big that turned up unexpectedly, we thought Fred Savory, our chief reporter. No one knows just how old Fred is; he keeps it dark, like his dyed black hair. He's a stocky, very muscular man, exuding vitality, and always immaculately dressed. He's reputed to spend hours in the reporters' room polishing his shoes and brushing his trouser bottoms. But I think he'd be good in a rumpus. He's a little spoiled after his years of service—expects the best jobs and normally gets them, and is frightfully good at wangling out-of-town assignments with high expenses, preferably abroad. In fact he has a cheek—but he's earned the right to it.

John Fletcher seemed the best man to talk to the yacht deliverer. John's a plump, cheerful, friendly person, only thirty or so but bald as an egg. He's a good mixer—and he's also taken some holidays on The Broads! It's the best we can do in the nautical line; our expert's in Bermuda. But at least John knows the front end of a boat from the back.

For direct work on Shirley Holt, we thought William Frost. Willie —another old stager, who's actually as tough as nails—has a quiet, amiable, gentlemanly approach, which soothes instead of scaring.

For the Franks Domestic Agency, and following up anything that arose from it, Edith Curtis seemed the best bet. She's homely, graying, doesn't look like a reporter, but she's a wise old hand at the game. She suffers from indigestion—not surprisingly. I've heard her order a strong black coffee, a vanilla ice cream, and a packet of charcoal biscuits from the canteen, all at the same time. But, indigestion or not, she does a good job.

After a quiet get-together with the News Editor—who'll need to make some big changes in his duty roster—Noll's going to have the reporters in for a briefing this evening.

The Prime Minister is being interviewed on B.B.C. TV tonight. I wonder what he'll have to say about the Lester affair. If he runs true to form, he'll be cagey.

And I wonder what the papers will have to say tomorrow about James's press conference. I'm nervous. There's a real danger that Shirley may become an object of public sympathy. In this country people do rally to the underdog—though in her case "dog" is possibly not the right word! She could so easily be represented as the ordinary, simple girl, first seduced and then repudiated by a lecherous, ambitious, and unscrupulous politician. After all, there have been politicians like that. By all accounts, several of the papers are definitely out to get James. You can almost hear the click of the needles as they wait for the head to roll.

10

SOURCE. Shorthand note by Linda Tandy of reporters' briefing by the Editor of the *Post.* News Editor and Night News Editor sitting in. Tuesday, April 17th. Extract.

". . . So that's the position as far as the News Room is concerned. Until further notice, work on the Lester case will have absolute priority over everything else, even if it means that we have to rely exclusively on agency copy for our ordinary news coverage.

"Well, I think that's about the lot—except that I'd like to reassure you on one final point. You all know that I'm a Lester man, and I know that some of you are, but maybe there are some of you who aren't. That's fine with me; your politics are no business of mine. What I don't want any of you to feel is that you're being conscripted into a pro-Lester campaign under the guise of reporting. We want the truth, wherever it may lead us. So just get the facts, and don't worry about the politics.

"Of course, on these assignments you'll be sending in confidential reports, not news stories, so the technique will be different from usual. We may publish bits of the information you collect, from time to time, and at the end of the day we may use the whole lot—who knows? But that isn't the object of the exercise. The object is to compile a comprehensive dossier on every aspect and angle of the Lester affair, so that we're as fully informed as it's possible to be. That means you can let yourselves go over background stuff in a way you'd never do with a news story—and I hope you will. I want to hear how your interviewees strike you as people, what their setup is, what their attitudes are to the case —in fact, everything that might conceivably help to fill in the picture. I'd also like you to make any comments of your own, friendly or unfriendly to Lester, that seem relevant. I stress that. If any of you get any bright ideas about the case as you go along, for goodness' sake don't sit on them—let me know. . . .

"One last point. We're very much up against the time factor in all this, so try to get on the blower as soon as you've got anything interesting. Don't feel you must wait until you can dictate a complete report on your whole assignment.

"That's all, then, and good hunting."

11

SOURCE. B.B.C. TV interview with the Prime Minister, the Rt.
Hon. David Cator, P.C., M.P. Interviewer Robert Angus.
Tuesday, April 17th. Extract.

"Have you any comment to make, Prime Minister, on the story that
seems likely to capture all the headlines in this election—Miss Holt's
allegations about the Leader of the Opposition, and Mr. Lester's denials?"

"Well, I hope you are wrong about the story capturing all the headlines—though I agree there are signs that it may happen. If so, I shall
regret it very much, and so will my colleagues. We want this election
to be fought on the political issues that divide us from the Opposition
party, as I'm quite sure the Leader of the Opposition does. I think it
would be a most damaging thing for the country if a purely personal
matter became a major issue—or, indeed, an issue at all. We are asking
the electorate for a renewal of our mandate on the basis of our record,
and that's what we intend to talk about."

"Would you not agree, though, that the personal integrity of a poten-
tial Prime Minister is a matter of proper concern to the electorate?"

"Mr. Angus, I prefer not to say anything more about this at all."

12

SOURCE. Editorial comment in the *Star.* Wednesday morning,
April 18th.

It would be foolish to pretend that there is now any issue of significance
in this election but the integrity of the man who a few days ago was
regarded as the certain victor and our next Prime Minister.

We all share the regrets expressed by Mr. Cator last night that this
should be so, but it is a fact that we have to accept. The country awaits
conclusive proof that Mr. Lester is a man whose word can be trusted.
So far, this proof is sadly lacking.

At a remarkable press conference yesterday, Mr. Lester, though outwardly frank, was less than convincing. Admittedly he came up with an
alternative version of what he was doing on the afternoon and night of
September 5th, but he was unable to produce any supporting testimony.
He was unable to suggest any reason why Miss Holt should have made
the allegations she has if they were not true; he was unable to advance
any explanation of how she knew so much about him and his yacht if
she had never met him; and he rejected out of hand the idea of a
confrontation.

For our part, we are reserving judgment until more facts become
available. But at least one of the statements made by Mr. Lester yesterday is likely to cause some eyebrow-raising. Asked why he could not
identify the flag of the motor cruiser which supposedly passed him in
the Sound of Mull, he said, "It was drooping round the pole, so I
couldn't make out what it was." Earlier he had told us that he was sailing
in "a fresh breeze." Does a flag droop in a fresh breeze?

13

SOURCE. Report to the *Post* by Fred Savory on his attempts to trace the hirers of the Oban speedboat. Wednesday, April 18th.

I telephoned the harbor master at Oban this morning and asked him if he could give me the names of local firms or yards who let out motor craft in the summer. He gave me three, and I hit pay dirt with the second one, J. B. McCulloch & Co. They said they had a 20-foot speedboat with two large Evinrude outboards, and they had hired it out for a few days early in September last year to two men from London. The actual hirer had been a Matthew Campbell, whose address was Flat 8, 24 Fortune Road, Kilburn.

I drove to Kilburn and found Fortune Road. It's a road of large tenement houses, fairly scruffy, though No. 24 is a little better than most. Flat 8 is on the second floor. There was no sign of life there, and from what I could see through the half-open letter slot—a scattering of circulars and a yellowing newspaper on the floor—there hadn't been for some time.

I knocked at all the doors in turn, but everyone was out at work, and it wasn't until nearly midday that I made a contact—a Mrs. Hooker, back with her shopping, who occupied Flat 6 below. But, oh, boy, was she a contact! She was a thin, bird-like woman, who'd obviously pecked around for every scrap of information she could collect. She knew just about everything, and it was quite a tale.

Matt Campbell, she said, had lived in Flat 8 with his wife, Becky, a brassy piece who had worked at a local hairdresser's. One of their rooms had been let out to another young man, Alf Haywood. Campbell and Haywood had been in business together, running a radio-controlled hire-car "fleet" of three or four cars with Pakistani drivers. It was this business, evidently, that they were "directors" of. They hadn't made much money at it, partly because Campbell was a hard drinker who didn't keep a proper eye on things. Mrs. H. had several times had to complain about the noise he made overhead when he was tight.

Then, in August last year, Matt and Alf had their big pools win— £23,000, Mrs. H. had heard. They sold their business, with its four jalopies, and Alf bought a new E-type Jaguar, and Becky packed up her job, and the three of them drove up to Scotland, where Campbell said his ancestors came from, though Mrs. H. reckoned it must have been a long way back. They got to Oban, and Becky settled down happily in a suite at the best hotel while the two lads hired their speedboat and lit out for Tobermory for a few days.

By the time they got back to London, Campbell was drinking harder than ever. He could afford the hard stuff now, and was on a punishing liquid diet most of the time. A month after their return, his friend Alf went off with Becky, leaving a brief note saying they were going to start a new life together in Australia and wouldn't be back. Nothing's been heard of them since.

I asked Mrs. H. what had happened to Campbell. She said he'd just gone on drinking, only more so, and one night he'd started to scream the place down, yelling that pink rats were chewing off his dingalings; and the police had been called and he'd been taken away, and for the past month he'd been getting over the d.t.'s in a Home for Inebriates in West End Lane.

I went to the Home and talked to the matron, explaining that I'd hoped Mr. Campbell might be a useful witness in a case my paper was interested in. She said she thought it very unlikely, but she let me see him. Campbell didn't seem in too bad shape physically, and he was friendly enough, but quite useless. He remembered falling into the drink at Tobermory, and he remembered talking to Lester after I'd described him, but he couldn't remember a word of anything that Lester had said, which wasn't surprising. Even if he had been able to, he'd have been no sort of a witness to produce to the press on Lester's behalf.

All in all, a dead loss, I'm afraid.

Okay if I fly out to Aussie to try and trace Alf and Becky?

14

SOURCE. Report to the *Post* by John Fletcher on an interview with the yacht deliverer Frank Jackson. Wednesday, April 18th.

Having telephoned Jackson last night to make sure he wasn't on the high seas, I drove to West Mersea early this morning, arriving at his place shortly before ten o'clock. The omens looked good from the start, because a newsboy was just pushing his morning paper through the letter box and I saw it was the *Post*. Jackson said he was a regular reader of the *Post* during his periods ashore, had been for years, and thought it easily the best value of any of the papers for fourpence. Which helped to get us on a friendly footing from the word go.

Jackson's home and place of business is an old black barge called *High Wind*, which is moored on saltings overlooking the Blackwater estuary and only floats at the highest spring tides. It's reached from the narrow coast road by a wooden catwalk raised over the mud. There's a roughly painted sign near the road—"Frank Jackson, Yacht Deliverer"—beside a platform, built out over the saltings, where he keeps his car.

As one would expect of a yacht deliverer, Jackson is a very tough, powerfully built man. He has enormous forearms, tattooed with anchors and fish. I gather he was in the merchant navy before he set up in the delivery business. He's quite handsome in a weather-beaten sort of way —blue eyes wrinkled at the corners, strong jaw, fetching grin. I'd guess he's about forty. I wouldn't think he'd ever had much formal education but he's intelligent, practical, and interesting to talk to.

His barge is roomy and comfortable inside. There's a big saloon, well-lit by skylights and by a large window he had installed at the seaward end to give him a view over the water. His furniture looks like a hodge-podge of sale bargains, but he's got everything he needs for living and for his work. The place is pretty well cluttered with nautical stuff— charts, almanacs, barometers, books of sailing directions, piles of old yachting journals, and so on. It's very much a male setup, with no sign of any female around. Later in our talk, when we were getting on extremely well, I asked him if he didn't ever feel the need of a woman around the place to look after him. He said no, he was used to it; he'd been mending his own socks and doing his own dhobying all his life, and he reckoned the disadvantages of having a wife around were a lot greater than the advantages. He added with a grin that when you had a girl in every port you really didn't need a woman at home. I'll bet he's broken a few hearts in his time!

Anyway, so much for the background. Now to business.

Jackson remembered Lester very well. He'd read an account of the press conference in yesterday's evening paper, and the unusual name of Lester's boat, *Raradoa,* had brought it all back to him. He himself had been collecting a yacht, he said, from Arinagour on the Island of Coll, and had called in at Tobermory to make a small repair, and was berthed at the same quay as Lester. He said he and Lester had yarned together quite a bit, and that he'd enjoyed meeting him. He'd found him a pretty knowledgeable sailor for an amateur, and a very decent bloke. Of course, he hadn't had any notion then what a big shot Lester was going to become.

I told him we were looking for supporting witnesses, and asked him if he could confirm any of the information Lester had given at the press conference. He said he could confirm practically all of it. Lester had not only told him he was leaving for Oban that night, he had also suggested Jackson should occupy his vacant berth, because a ship was coming in to unload and Jackson was due to move his own boat on the tide late that afternoon to make room for it. In fact, Jackson *had* occupied the berth. He was quite surprised to find Lester back at the quay next morning, and asked him what had happened, and was told about the abortive trip through the Sound and shown the bit of rope that had clogged Lester's propeller. He didn't think Lester had mentioned the motor cruiser at the time, but otherwise his story had been very much the same as the one he'd told at the press conference.

I asked Jackson what he thought about the case in general. He said —but in rather more pungent words—that he hadn't the slightest doubt Lester was telling the truth and the girl was lying. I asked him why he felt so sure, since he couldn't know for certain whether Lester had actually attempted the passage or not. He said he knew bloody well! Again I asked him why. He said because of Lester's statement about not being able to identify the flag at the stern of the motor cruiser because it was drooping. I thought I couldn't have heard properly! I told him that one of the papers that morning had taken an exactly opposite view and had asked nastily how a flag could be drooping in a fresh breeze. He said that just showed what an ignorant lot of landlubbers they were. If Lester had had a head wind, as he'd said, that meant the cruiser going the other way had had the wind with it, and if the cruiser was doing fifteen knots and the wind was blowing about the same speed, there'd have been a flat calm around the ship and the flag *would* have been drooping.

So much for the nautical expertise of the *Star!*

Of course, I suppose it could be argued that a man of Lester's sailing experience would have had this point in mind at the press conference; that if he'd been describing a passage that he'd never made and a cruiser that he'd never encountered, he'd have had the knowledge and the sense to make sure that the technical facts he gave were consistent with each other—as apparently they now are. Probably that's what Lester's enemies *will* argue. All the same, I have the feeling that thanks to Jackson we've won a useful trick.

I had to finish there, because Jackson got tied up on the phone about some delivery. But I'd got what we wanted, and more. He'll be a first-class witness, if and when we need him—friendly to Lester and *ruggedly* independent.

15

SOURCE. Report to the *Post* by Edith Curtis on an interview with
Mrs. Ursula Field, manageress of the Franks Domestic Agency,
Berkeley Street, W. 1. Wednesday, April 18th.

Mrs. Field had already refused several requests for interviews by other reporters when I called on her. I thought at first she was going to turn me down, too, but she changed her mind after I'd sent in a persuasive note. I wrote that my paper was seeking to collect every scrap of information bearing on the Lester case, not primarily for publication, but because many of us believed Mr. Lester to be innocent of the charges leveled against him by Miss Holt, and perhaps what Mrs. Field could tell us might help in the campaign to clear him. I was gambling on whose side she was on, and the gamble paid off.

Mrs. Field is a smart, attractive woman of about fifty, with a crisp manner and a positive personality. She began by emphasizing that the agency never in any circumstances gave information to the press about its clients, but added that as Miss Holt had now been taken off their books and herself had talked freely to the press, the rule no longer applied to her.

I asked Mrs. Field first if she knew anything about Shirley's background. She said certainly she did, because an agency of repute couldn't recommend anyone they hadn't thoroughly investigated. Shirley had come of a very good family. Her father had been an airline pilot, with a distinguished war record behind him. Her mother had been a social worker. Both parents had died when she was about twenty, her father in some kind of flying accident. She had come to the agency with excellent references, one from the Mother Superior at the convent school where she had been educated. She had seemed in every way the sort of person a high-class agency would welcome.

I asked Mrs. Field if she would mind telling me which convent school, and she got out Shirley's file and said it was the Convent of the Sacred Heart at Heathfield, Sussex. She said she couldn't disclose what the Mother Superior had said in the letter, since it was confidential, but perhaps I might be able to see her myself—which I shall certainly try to do.

I then asked about Shirley's record as a children's nurse. How had she turned out? How had she rated? Mrs. Field said that if I'd asked her that question a few days earlier, she'd have given a glowing account of Shirley. In the four years she'd been on their books, she'd proved a splendid children's nurse—kind, willing, good-tempered, and helpful in every way. There'd been innumerable tributes and commendations from employers, and hardly a word of criticism.

I said, if there had been *some* criticism, what had it been about? Mrs. Field (trying hard, I felt, to be fair) said that some people were never satisfied. There had been a letter praising Shirley for her kindness, willingness, good temper, and so on, but saying that she never appeared really *interested* in the children she looked after, and that it was rather as though she were keeping an amiable eye on small animals. But that letter had been quite exceptional. The fact was that Shirley had given tremendous satisfaction almost everywhere, and toward the end had been in the privileged position of being able to pick her jobs according to her fancy. There was, of course, a considerable demand for top-class children's nurses by wealthy people—not just on a permanent basis, but for the shorter periods like school holidays and wintering abroad and so on, which was what Shirley preferred, because she liked change and travel.

I then asked Mrs. Field how she felt about the recent happenings. She said she had to look at it in two ways—professional and personal. From the agency point of view, there could be only one attitude. The almost worldwide notoriety that Shirley had brought on herself by her own statements made it quite improbable that anyone would again want to employ her as a children's nurse. Certainly the agency would have found it quite impossible to recommend her. Unfortunately (and here a note of bitterness crept in) it wasn't only Shirley's reputation that had been harmed by all the publicity, but to some extent the agency's as well.

I said, "And what about your personal view of events? How do you see the rights and wrongs of the case?"

She said, "Well, I'm a woman of the world, not a prude, and if a girl wants to have an affair and conducts it discreetly, good luck to her. But I find it impossible to condone Shirley's behavior. Even if her story is true, I can't see that it was necessary for her to tell it in such detail and with such apparent relish. She seems to me to be flaunting her unorthodox conduct. And of course if her story isn't true, she must be a very wicked young woman indeed. On the whole my sympathies are with Mr. Lester, and I hope very much that things will come right for him."

She was silent for a moment. Then she gave a sort of final summing-up. She said that in the past day or two she'd reflected a good deal about Shirley, and had come to the conclusion that while her professional behavior had been outwardly impeccable, it had perhaps been slightly automatic. Shirley was a withdrawn rather than an outgoing girl, never showing much emotion, never reacting very much, in fact appearing rather insensitive to outside influences and events. So that after four years of quite close dealings with her, it was difficult to feel that one *knew* her. And now of course it was apparent that one hadn't really known her at all.

I said I was very interested in those last remarks, about Shirley being withdrawn rather than outgoing. In considering whether or not her story was true, we had come up right away against an apparent total lack of motive for making false allegations, and we'd naturally wondered about her mental state. On further reflection, and with the advantage of hindsight, could Mrs. Field recall anything at any time in Shirley's attitude or behavior that suggested any kind of mental instability? Mrs. Field was quite emphatic that she had meant nothing of that kind. She had merely been trying to describe a certain kind of personality. There was no question in her view of any mental or emotional disturbance. Shirley had always seemed a very stable and equable girl.

I thanked Mrs. Field for her most helpful interview, and promised on the *Post*'s behalf that we wouldn't print anything she'd said without first getting her permission.

Afterthoughts by E. C.:

1. Mrs. Field considers she has been very badly let down, and at heart she's much more anti-Shirley than the interview suggests. I felt that with her later reflections she was perhaps trying to fit Shirley's character to events, rather than the other way round.

2. It did occur to me at one stage during the interview that the picture of Shirley as a professional children's nurse, with all those excellent qualities, was almost too good to be true. Didn't she *ever* lose her temper, sulk, do something unkind? Was she *always* placid? If so, could this be a case of still waters? One wonders. But of course it may be that temperamentally she's just a born children's nurse.

3. One thing stands out a mile. It's clear that Shirley has managed to talk herself out of a steady, well-paid, and interesting career which she appeared to enjoy, and after all the publicity she could well have trouble in earning a decent living at anything for quite a while. She must surely have known this would happen when she started talking so freely to the press—so in a way it supports her case. Would she have thrown everything up just for the pleasure of telling a whopping lie?

Note for News Editor

I have made an appointment with the Mother Superior at the Sacred Heart convent school, and am now driving down to Sussex to see her.

16

SOURCE. Report to the *Post* by Edith Curtis on an interview with the Mother Superior at the Convent of the Sacred Heart, Heathfield, Sussex. Wednesday, April 18th.

The Sacred Heart boarding school is a complex of rather dreary nineteenth-century buildings, but it is set in lovely spacious grounds with open views. Mother Mary is a woman of sixty or so, very alert, with bright blue eyes and shiny pink cheeks. I told her of our special interest in the Lester case, and she said she had naturally followed it closely herself. She remembered Shirley Holt well, though it was now eight years or more since Shirley had left school. "She was a beautiful girl," Mother Mary said, "with the face of an angel."

We had a long and friendly conversation, from which the following main points emerged:

1. Shirley's parents had not been Catholics, but the father in particular had favored a convent education for his daughter—an only child, by the way—and the mother had thought she would enjoy a boarding school in the country. Mother Mary had met both parents, but only on one or two occasions, so she had never got to know them well. Captain Holt had been a handsome and impressive man, rather quiet; Mrs. Holt had done most of the talking and discussing. Both of them had been

busy career people. Captain Holt had his flying duties, and Mrs. Holt was employed by some public body to visit people in their homes and advise and help them. A very worthy occupation, Mother Mary said—always provided, she added, that one's own home was not deprived of proper care and affection as a result.

2. Shirley never paid a visit to the school after she'd left, and for a year or two she was lost sight of. Then, four or five years ago, a letter arrived from her. In it she said, in a fairly laconic way, that her father had been killed flying a light aircraft in bad weather, and that her mother had died of cancer after a short illness, and that she herself had been traveling and doing various little jobs, but that she now wanted something more permanent and thought she would enjoy being a children's nurse, and could Mother Mary give her a reference? Which Mother Mary had been very happy to do. Shirley had sent a brief note of thanks, and there had been no further word from her.

3. I asked about Shirley's school career—what her special interests had been, and so on. Mother Mary said she'd been a clever girl but not brilliant academically. She'd done well in most subjects without showing any outstanding interest in any particular one. She'd been averagely keen on games and averagely popular with the other girls. One of her outside interests, Mother Mary recalled, had been the school dramatic society —but no hasty conclusions should be drawn from that, because amateur acting was popular with lots of young girls. As far as behavior was concerned, Shirley had been an amenable and docile girl, and had given no trouble at all.

4. I asked Mother Mary how, on reflection, she would describe Shirley's character as she remembered it. She thought for a moment or two, and then said that perhaps her detachment was what came most to mind —a lack of deep involvement with anyone or anything. She had been a very self-contained girl, a little withdrawn on occasion—but only a little. Certainly not in any serious clinical sense. There had never been the slightest sign of mental disturbance.

5. I said that one reporter who'd talked to Shirley had described her as "a composed, gentle, amiable girl, rather unworldly, and in some

matters quite naïve." Mother Mary thought this a pretty perceptive description on short acquaintance, and didn't quarrel with it as far as it went.

So there we are: a lot of words about Shirley from two people who knew her well—a lot of thought, too—and the picture that emerges is pretty consistent. Unfortunately it's a picture that throws little or no light on whether she's now telling the truth or lying. I feel I've got rather laboriously nowhere!

17

SOURCE. Report to the *Post* by George Bromley on inquiries made on the Island of Mull. Wednesday, April 18th. Report telephoned at 10:30 P.M.

I flew to Glasgow early this morning as arranged. The chartered helicopter picked me up on schedule and I was in Tobermory by midday.

I talked first to the harbor master. He is a retired submarine commander named Ferguson and a very pleasant fellow. Naturally he had read all about the Lester case, which has aroused particularly strong interest up here because of the local connections and has been fully reported in the Oban *Times*. He remembered Lester very well, and the boat *Raradoa*, and had already looked up his records for his own satisfaction. In addition to his official records, he keeps a private log, over and above the call of duty, because he became accustomed to doing this during his service in submarines. He was therefore well prepared to discuss the matter, which we did over a couple of pink gins.

He confirmed that Mr. Lester's boat was at the quay on September 5th last year, and recalled that he had had several talks with Lester and had also been invited aboard *Raradoa* for a drink. He had an entry in his records that *Raradoa* had left Tobermory soon after midday on the fifth, and a further entry that a Mr. Jackson, in *Spindrift*, would be occupying Lester's berth not later than 5 P.M. that day to make room for a vessel called *Highland Lassie* to go alongside and discharge cargo. He remembered that Mr. Lester had told him he proposed to anchor offshore for a few hours and then sail for Oban on the night tide. He had looked up the tides and the meteorological reports for September 5th, and they were in accordance with Mr. Lester's public statements.

Ferguson was also able to confirm, from his records, that *Raradoa* had reappeared at Tobermory on the morning of September 6th. He hadn't seen her enter harbor, but had spotted her tied up at a vacant berth around 9 A.M. Mr. Lester had told him that he had had engine trouble on his way to Oban and had thought it wiser to return.

I asked the commander what his own views were about the case. He shrugged and said that, having seen the very attractive Miss Holt being interviewed on TV last night, he wouldn't like to make a bet either way. He added, with a grin, that in Lester's position he'd have admitted everything and proposed marriage. I said that my experience of marriage was that it was a mistake. On a more serious note, the commander did say that he had thought Mr. Lester "a very straightforward chap."

Ferguson is very alert and on the ball and would make a good witness to Mr. Lester's expressed intentions and the statements he made on his return, though of course he has no idea whether *Raradoa* actually did attempt the passage to Oban.

I subsequently proceeded to the Island Motel to inquire about Miss Holt's stay there. The motel is a fairly new enterprise. It is situated near the cliff top on the northern outskirts of Tobermory, with a pleasant view of the sea. The man at the desk was not at all useful at first, being very Scottish (from Dundee) and difficult to understand, as well as seeming reluctant to talk. However, after some exchanges and the use of signs, we found a common interest in racing, and I was able to show him how Happy Returns had been practically bound to win the Stirling Stakes, on form and with the ground soft and with Prescott riding, and

I explained my system and he was very intrigued. He then looked up the motel records for the previous September and was able to confirm that Miss Holt had checked in at the motel on September 3rd and had checked out on the morning of September 6th. He could not say whether or not she had spent the night of September 5th at the motel, since the rooms were remote from the porter's lodge, and even if anyone had noticed at the time, which was unlikely, it was now too long ago for anyone to remember. I suggested that he should look to see if Miss Holt had taken a meal in the restaurant that evening, but he said they only had a cafeteria where meals were paid for on the spot, so there were no records, and it would be impossible for anyone to say now whether Miss Holt had eaten at the cafeteria or not. This was all rather disappointing, as a positive answer would have been most useful to our case.

I then took a stroll round the motel and had a look at room No. 14, the one to which Miss Holt had been assigned. It is at the extreme end of a block, well away from the public rooms, and I formed the view that she could easily have gone in or out at any time without any special notice of her being taken. I considered trying to get the names and addresses of people who had occupied rooms in the same block at the same period, but the chance that anyone would remember seeing a particular person around on a particular evening seven months ago was so remote that I decided against it.

I subsequently visited the cove (it is named as Frian Cove on the ordnance survey map) which Miss Holt has indicated to reporters as being the one where she alleges she met Mr. Lester. It is accessible only by a rough, steep track from the minor moorland road above it, or else by walking some three miles from Tobermory along the cliff top. It has a sandy beach, shut in by high rocky headlands on both sides, and it certainly is a very secluded place where one could expect to sunbathe undisturbed.

Finally, after lengthy inquiries, I was able to confirm this evening that Miss Holt was resident for a few weeks last summer as children's nurse to a family who rented a villa named Bonnie Doon, just outside Tobermory and close to the golf links.

I was unable to confirm whether or not Miss Holt did in fact catch the steamer to Oban on the morning of September 6th. There are no passenger lists for these short journeys and too much time has elapsed for anyone to remember seeing her.

18

SOURCE. Report to the *Post* by William Frost on his interview with Shirley Holt at 37 Egerton Road, Surbiton. Wednesday, April 18th. Telephoned to the *Post* at 12 noon.

I was a little surprised to find Shirley still staying at her flat, in view of all the publicity she has received and the inevitable unpleasantness with some neighbors—not to mention the almost hourly visits of newsmen and the constant telephone calls. But she is sticking it out, and seems astonishingly unaffected by all the hullabaloo. She gives the impression of being indifferent to criticism because she is sustained by a sense of right and justice. She is turning out to be a much stronger and more stubborn character than early descriptions would have suggested. Her line is that she's been called a liar publicly, which she isn't, and she's not going to run away just because Jim Lester is a clever man with powerful friends. So she'll continue to be available to the press at her flat—at least, she said, as long as her savings last. The flat, though modest enough and in an unfashionable area, is comfortably furnished, and must cost her every penny of fifteen pounds a week. She could afford to have it when she was earning, she said; and of course she had to have a base somewhere to return to between jobs and to keep her belongings in and for contacts with the agency. But now she's out of work it's obviously going to be more difficult for her.

I must say she seemed to me a very courageous girl—and she's quite stunning to look at; she'd turn any man's head. But she's not at all flirtatious; there's no come-hither stuff about her. In fact she's rather serious.

One interesting item of news is that she, too, has now sworn an affidavit! It was the *Clarion*'s idea. Apparently their man Harker called on her last night with a draft statement based on what she'd told the press, and convinced her it would enormously strengthen her case in the eyes of the public if she swore to the truth of it, as Lester had done with his story, so this morning she went off with him to a Commissioner of Oaths and did the job there and then. Harker borrowed the document to photograph, and still has it, so it's the *Clarion*'s scoop and they'll no doubt be using it tomorrow. One thing's now clear: at the end of the day, *someone* is going to jail for perjury. Whatever one's view of the rights and wrongs, it's a fascinating struggle.

By the way, I asked Shirley how *she* felt about a public confrontation with Lester—which he, of course, has refused. She said she wasn't awfully keen on the idea, because it would be rather horrid meeting him again like that after what had happened between them, but she wouldn't say no if he changed his mind and wanted to. She didn't think he would, though; she didn't think he'd be able to repeat his denials, face to face, and that he knew this and wouldn't risk it.

Now to the specific matters I called on Shirley to discuss.

She was completely forthcoming when I asked her about her movements during the past seven months. She got out her engagement book and gave me the following detailed account:

She was with the Tancred family at Tobermory from August 3rd last to September 3rd. Their London address—for confirmation, if required —is 32 Mount Crescent, W. 1. She was at the Island Motel from September 3rd to September 6th, when she caught the steamer to Oban and continued by train directly to London, arriving September 7th. She spent two days at her flat getting ready for her next job, and on September 10th was picked up by car by the Devereux family (address: 3 Sloane

Mews, S.W. 3) and traveled with them to Saint-Jean-de-Luz, near Biarritz. She was with them until November 1st, when she left to take up her next engagement. She was met in Bordeaux on November 3rd by the Barbers (address: 13 Sherborne Road, St. John's Wood, N.W. 8), a retired couple with two small grandchildren to look after (bad divorce trouble in the family), and taken to Monte Gordo in the Portuguese Algarve for the winter. She was with the Barbers till March 3rd, when she left for Menton on the French Riviera, arriving there on March 5th to join a French woman, Mme. Renée Laporte (address: 14 *bis*, Boulevard Henri Quatre, Paris), and her twelve-year-old invalid son (main job to improve his English). She left Menton on April 9th, stopped off in Paris for a day or two to do some shopping, and returned to England by the night-train ferry on April 12th, arriving on the morning of April 13th and hoping (she said) "for a good rest."

I now switched to the subject of Lester's boat and asked her if she could give me a more detailed description of some of its contents, as her first account had been rather general. She said several reporters had already asked her the same question, so she had a mental list all ready. She mentioned a chromium-plated barometer and clock; a book called *The Western Isles of Scotland;* a card, pinned up with drawing pins, which she said Lester had told her was a tide table; a sailing ship in a bottle; a coil of green rope; and a green-and-white woolen bobble cap. I asked her to tell me, if she could, where these things had been in the cabin, and she said the clock and barometer were mounted just inside the cabin, one on each side of the door, and the book was in a small bookrack, and the ship in a bottle was in a locker under one of the bunks, and the rope had been somewhere in "the front part," and she couldn't remember where the bobble cap had been—she thought in another locker. The card had been pinned up under the barometer by the door. She added one other item of information that she'd only just remembered: there'd been a button missing from the left-hand bunk cover, just where you sat down.

Assuming her facts prove correct, it seems to me we now have to rule out altogether the possibility that Shirley got her description of the interior of the boat merely by looking in from the quay. Many of these things—certainly the barometer and the clock, the pinned card, the ship in the bottle, and probably the book—would have been invisible to anyone just glancing in through the door. And *either* the barometer *or* the clock (depending on how the boat lay) would have been invisible to anyone looking in through a window, as would the pinned card, the ship in the bottle, and the title of the book. My conclusion is that either Shirley was in the cabin at some time or she has talked to someone who was.

I feel it is a point to note in her favor that she didn't herself advance this rather vital information at the start of the case, but has had to have it extracted from her by newsmen bit by bit.

I next raised the point mentioned by Miss Tandy about Shirley having apparently given her address to Lester and him not reciprocating, and I asked her if she hadn't thought this an awful snub.

She looked at me in a surprised way, as though the thought simply hadn't occurred to her. Then she said, "Oh, I see!" And she explained that it hadn't been like that at all. The only reason she'd given Lester her address, she said, was that at the last minute she'd discovered that she'd lost something on the boat, and she'd scribbled the address down so that if he found it he could send it on, and there'd been no question of reciprocating.

I asked her what it was she had lost, and she said it was the stone from a ring she'd been wearing—a small amber-colored topaz. She said the ring wasn't particularly valuable—it was really like a piece of costume jewelry—but it had been her mother's, so she felt a bit sentimental about it. I asked her if she still had the ring and, if so, whether I could see it, and she searched in a couple of handbags and finally produced it. It was a rather heavy ring of—I think—silver (chased? filigree?—something like that), and I could see that the clasps that had held the stone were very worn down. Shirley said she'd been silly to go on wearing the ring, because she'd noticed the topaz was a bit loose and she should have had it seen to. Anyway, she said, she'd never heard from Lester, so she supposed he hadn't found the stone, which wasn't surprising considering how tiny it was. For all she knew, it was still somewhere at the bottom of his boat.

She seemed rather concerned that people should think she hadn't minded being snubbed and said she must remember to tell the other reporters about the ring. With all the hoopla, she'd completely forgotten about the incident until now.

I should think there'll be quite a stampede of newsmen to look over Lester's boat today!

19

SOURCE. Linda Tandy's diary. Wednesday, April 18th.

2 P.M.

Noll and I were rather pleased with the first reports we got today. The yacht deliverer's contribution could hardly have been better, and Noll is going to use part of it in the *Post* tomorrow. The speedboat hirers were a flop, of course, but with Jackson (and, we hope, the harbor master) on our side, that doesn't matter. And Edith's agency report was at least fairly neutral.

Then Willie Frost's piece came in—which was a bit of a setback. At least, it seemed so at first.

Neither of us doubts that Shirley's detailed description of *Raradoa*'s cabin arrangements will prove accurate in every respect when James checks it. Obviously she wouldn't have dared to be so specific if she hadn't been sure. Noll says he hadn't himself noted the bobble cap or the ship in the bottle or the missing button when he was on board, but other people could have been more observant. From his own knowledge he can vouch for the rest of the items.

I asked him if he thought Shirley could possibly have got into the cabin sometime without James's knowledge. He said definitely not. James always locked up if he was going to be away for more than a few minutes, especially in harbor—and the sort of inventory Shirley had produced would have taken quite a while to collect.

So that leaves us with Willie's alternative—that Shirley got her information from someone else, who *was* aboard at some time. Which merely faces us with a great big query. In addition to the several people at Tobermory who were probably invited aboard and whom we definitely know about—the harbor master, the yacht deliverer, the speedboat hirers, the grocery man, and so on—there are countless unknown casuals. Noll says that in the few days he was cruising the islands, at least four other yachtsmen came aboard *Raradoa* for a drink, and the same thing would have gone on with James on his own—probably more so. Noll says what happens is that a fellow yachtsman stops to admire your boat at a quay, or rows over at an anchorage, and you exchange a few friendly words with him, and then you naturally ask him aboard for a look round—not to do so would be like keeping an acquaintance standing on your doorstep instead of asking him in. And of course they always accept, because there's nothing a yachtsman likes so much as looking over someone else's boat, except perhaps showing his own—and then you suggest a drink, and you chat, and they finally push off and you never see them again. It's all routine, part of the fun, and it goes on all the time. In short, so many people would have been in that cabin of James's, exchanging views about comparative fittings and fixtures and yarning their heads off about being caught out in Force 9 gales and clawing off lee shores, that we could almost as well try to seek them out by sticking a pin in the telephone directory.

All the same, Willie's report has carried things forward a little. It's hard to believe that Shirley got all that information by chance from some entirely uninvolved person, and then used it for a solo operation. Which means she's in collusion with somebody. It follows, doesn't it? *Doesn't it?*

As for the topaz story, it's obvious that she invented that on the spur of the moment, to fill a gap in her first statement that she'd overlooked. She's resourceful—there's no doubt about that. And crafty. She must know that such a tiny thing could never be found at the bottom of a boat, so she's safe to talk about it.

Noll is sending Fred Savory to see the new owner of the boat, but it's pure routine. As Shirley was never on the boat, she *couldn't* have lost a topaz there. . . .

If only I could get rid of this creeping fear . . .

20

SOURCE. Report by Fred Savory on his visit to the new owner of
James Lester's boat. Wednesday, April 18th. Afternoon. Report
telephoned to the *Post*, 6 P.M.

I got the new owner's name and address from the *Registry of Yachts* without any trouble. It is William Haines, of Green Boughs, Oakfield Road, Walton-on-the-Naze, Essex. Thanks to the flying start given me by Willie Frost, I was the first newsman to reach Walton on this latest angle.

Haines lives in a detached house with a large walled garden, overlooking one of the backwaters behind the town. I didn't have to ask him where the boat was. It was right there in the garden, laid up under a tarpaulin.

Haines is a local builder—and a pretty prosperous one, judging by the appearance of his place. He's a well-built, good-looking chap, in his early forties, I'd say. He has a jolly but incredibly fat wife, a good bit older than himself. They have a couple of teen-age daughters, whom I didn't meet; they're at boarding school in Eastbourne.

At the moment, Haines has his right leg in plaster up to the thigh, and stumps about with the help of crutches. He broke the leg on a solo skiing holiday at Chamonix in January—a very bad double fracture, he said. He has already had one operation and may have to have another. He is an active and vigorous man and is very fed up about the whole business.

Lester's boat was delivered to his home by a local firm shortly after he got back from Chamonix. He had arranged to have it laid up for the winter in his garden, rather than in a boatyard, because he was planning to make some small structural changes to the cabin before fitting out in the spring. His accident knocked that plan on the head, as he wouldn't even be able to climb aboard, but, having made the arrangement and prepared the site, he thought he might as well go ahead and have the boat there, ready for when he was fit again.

Haines and his wife have, naturally, been following the Lester saga with special interest. He has been approached by quite a few reporters in the past day or two, and has talked to them, but he's refused to allow any of them to look over *Raradoa* because of the business of getting it out of wraps. He was most intrigued when I told him what Shirley Holt had said about a lost topaz, though he still wasn't keen to open up the boat. But by now more newsmen were arriving, all of them set on a treasure hunt, and when there were eight of us he gave in and said okay, but warned that the work would be heavy and that we'd have to do all of it ourselves and leave everything shipshape afterward. He then stumped ahead of us to the boat.

Raradoa was standing upright on its twin bilge keels, and was raised a foot or so from the ground on balks of timber. It had been placed very close to the garden wall and could therefore only be approached comfortably from one side. Its mast had been taken out, and the top two-thirds of the hull was covered from end to end with a green canvas tarpaulin, lashed down with ropes that went under the boat. We undid the lashings at the stern end—the knots were stiff, and it took the better part of fifteen minutes—and then someone brought a ladder from Haines's shed, which was the only way you could climb to the cockpit. As it was clear we couldn't all inspect the boat at once, we agreed that the first three of us who'd arrived should represent the others. Haines obviously couldn't get up himself, and neither could Mrs. H.—she said, with a big laugh, that it was all she could do to climb her own doorstep! Haines gave me the cabin key, and wired up an inspection lamp on a long cable from the shed. The three of us then climbed up—myself; Gerry Fox, of the *Telegraph;* and Wiltshire, a P.A. photographer—and stood balanced on the side deck, hanging on to stanchions covered by the canvas.

The tarpaulin had collected a pool of rainwater in a sag over the cockpit, dirtied by twigs and dead leaves and bird droppings from the trees above. There was a surprising amount of water, considering the drought there's been this spring. Most of it must have come from those heavy rains we had toward the end of January. You could see where the pool had gradually receded through evaporation, leaving a succession of dark concentric marks on the canvas, the outer ring being very sharp. The tarpaulin clearly hadn't been disturbed for months.

Wiltshire took several pictures of the pool, and then the three of us hauled up a corner of the tarpaulin—which was much heavier and more difficult to handle than it looked—and squeezed ourselves into the cockpit. Someone passed up the lamp, and I unlocked the cabin door. The lock was a Chubb in good working order, very strong and pretty well burglarproof. The woodwork around it, and the fastenings, showed no sign of having been tampered with.

I went inside with the lamp while the other two watched from the door. Lester had taken most of his belongings out of the boat at the time of the sale and the cabin was pretty well empty, but the berth covers had been left in place—and one of them *does* have a button missing.

Between us, we went over every inch of that boat, taking turns because the work was heavy. We had all the floorboards up, and examined the gaps between the lumps of iron ballast, and had quite a bit of it out so we could inspect the bilges. We examined the lockers under the bunks, and the shelves above, the cupboards and the bookrack, the gas cooker and its surroundings, the washbasin and loo—though I imagined if anything as small as a topaz had been dropped down either of those it would have been washed away long ago—and finally the cockpit itself and all its lockers. We must have been at it for an hour and a half before we finally gave up. Of course we knew it had been a long shot from the beginning, and no one was very surprised when we didn't find anything.

We were on the point of heaving the tarpaulin back when Foster, of the *Mail*, called up that his wife had once lost a ring down a washbasin waste pipe and it had stuck in a U-bend, and had we looked to see if there was one? I went back in and had a second look at the basin. The plughole had a couple of protective crosspieces just inside it, presumably to prevent that very thing, but the gaps were large enough to let a small jewel through. I looked under the basin, and there *was* a U-bend, with a hexagonal cap at the bottom that you could unscrew in case the pipe got blocked. The cap was covered with white paint and looked as though it hadn't been touched since the basin was installed. I waited while Haines got some tools from the shed, and then—after a heck of a struggle and some barked knuckles—I loosened the cap and screwed it off. A few drops of dirty water came out, but nothing else. I put a finger into the hole and felt around—and a moment later I brought out a small amber-colored topaz.

That was a real sensation for one and all. There was a rush up the ladder, and everyone was jabbering, and flashes were going off from all directions. In twenty years of reporting, I've never known anything quite like it. Haines himself was staggered by the discovery—and pretty appalled, realizing what it meant for Lester. He was absolutely emphatic that no one had been aboard the boat since it had been delivered and laid up in January—though he hardly needed to tell us, because of the evidence of the pool of rainwater.

I put the cap back, and tightened it, and we cleared everything up, locked the door, hauled back the tarpaulin, roped it up, and returned the ladder to the shed. Haines said we'd better leave the topaz with him, which we did after it had been examined, measured, and photographed from every angle.

I don't know how Jim Lester's going to talk himself out of this one!

21

SOURCE. Linda Tandy's diary. Wednesday, April 18th.

The finding of the topaz this afternoon came as a frightful shock. James couldn't be reached on the telephone, so Noll sent a copy of Fred Savory's report by hand to his HQ, with an urgent request that James should be contacted, and we waited for him to ring the office. He came through shortly after seven o'clock. Noll talked to him, and I listened in on the extension.

James was in a great rush to get to a meeting and couldn't talk for long. His tone was sharper than usual. He said the topaz must have been planted, it couldn't have got into the boat any other way, and it was now clear he was being made the target of a determined conspiracy. Noll tried to be practical and helpful, going over with him the boat's precise movements since Tobermory, trying to find out what opportunities there might have been for anyone to plant the stone. James couldn't think of any; in fact, he said flatly there couldn't have been any during the time he was the owner. He said that the boat had been left at Oban with a very reliable yard, as Noll knew; that it had been left locked up with its foolproof lock; that he had kept the only two keys in his own possession, since there was no reason why anyone at the yard should want to enter the cabin; and that if an entry had been forced at any time, then or later, it would certainly have been apparent. After Oban, the boat had been brought south by road, still locked up, with the keys still in James's possession, and had been put in a marina on the Essex Blackwater where there was a day-and-night watchman. When Haines had shown an interest in its purchase, James had met him and his surveyor at the marina, opened the boat up for them, stayed with them throughout the inspection, and subsequently locked it again. Haines had been satisfied, and they'd settled the deal then and there. Haines had written out a check and James had handed over the keys—and that was the end of his knowledge. He was completely baffled by what had happened; but it was, he repeated, definitely a plant. He'd give the problem some thought as soon as he had a moment, and he'd get in touch with us again.

That, for the time being, was James's whole contribution. As an exercise in the wholesale slamming of doors, it was magnificent. Only a consciously innocent man, I thought, would have dismissed so many possibilities so fast. But it wasn't very constructive.

After he'd rung off, Noll and I began an anxious discussion about it all. It was easy enough for James to say in a vague sort of way that the topaz must have been planted, but the *when* and the *how* and the *by whom* were vital if anyone but us was going to believe it. Noll said he was sure James was right about its not having been done while he owned the boat—not only because of the evidence about the keys and the intact door, though that was pretty conclusive, but because of the point he himself had raised a day or two back in connection with Shirley's possible motive: that no one would have gone to the trouble of concocting a complex plot against James at a time when he was of minor national importance. One way and another, therefore, one could probably rule out a planting before the sale. So where did that leave us?

It left us, obviously, with Haines, the man who had taken over and had had charge of the boat for the rest of the time. Haines, about whom we so far knew almost nothing. Now Haines moved into the center of our spotlight, and at once a host of questions began to suggest themselves. We drew up a list—not in any special order, just as the points occurred to us—and by the time we'd exhausted our ideas it went something like this:

1. Had Haines retained possession of the boat keys after James had handed them over to him, or had he given them to the people who were to deliver the boat, or the marina people, or anyone else?

2. In spite of superficial appearances to the contrary, would it have been possible for someone to have got in under the tarpaulin after it had been placed in position, planted the topaz, and refixed the cover as though it hadn't been touched?

We gave a lot of thought to this, and came up with the following conclusions:

a.   It might have been possible if there had been a dry period after the delivery of the boat and before the first rain fell, when the tarpaulin could have been turned back and the cabin entered by key without any traces being left.

b.   It might just have been possible immediately after the first rain, before the sharp outer ring of the pool had formed. (Check weather and dates.)

c.   It would have been quite impossible once the ring had formed. Any disturbance of the tarpaulin, even the amount necessary to raise a corner and get into the cockpit, would also have disturbed the pool of dirty water and blurred the line of the outer concentric mark. And the pictures had shown that there hadn't been any blurring. Once the tarpaulin had been tampered with, no sort of faking could have restored the pool to the condition in which it had been first seen by reporters.

3. Leaving aside the considerable problem of how an intruder could have got hold of a key, could anyone have entered the boat and planted the topaz without Haines and/or his wife knowing about it? (In view of the closeness of the boat to the house, the heavy and far from silent work required to get the ropes untied and the wrappings off, the need for a ladder, the time it would have taken to do the job, and so on, we felt this would have been impossible while the Haineses were in residence. And they would hardly have gone away at a time when Haines was crippled by a badly broken leg. But this raised another question.)

4. *Had* Haines broken his leg? So far, we had no independent evidence of it. What was under that plaster? How long had the plaster been on? Who had put it on, and where? If the leg was broken, how bad was the injury? Could Haines, in spite of appearances, have climbed the ladder himself?

5. Did Haines know Shirley Holt? He was a youngish, good-looking, active man, married to a fat, much older wife—and he took holidays on his own. Could Shirley be his girl friend on the side? Had she given him the topaz at some time, for him to plant? Or posted it to him?

6. Assuming the leg injury was genuine, could Shirley herself have entered the cabin and planted the topaz, with Haines's connivance and help from the ground, on some occasion when Mrs. H. was out for a few hours? Had there been any gaps in the continuity of Shirley's engagements abroad which would have allowed her to pop back to England and do the job?

7. Was it from Haines that Shirley had got her detailed knowledge of the contents of the boat? He'd have seen James's belongings undisturbed when he'd gone with his surveyor to look over the vessel. He'd have had all the lockers open. He'd have examined everything.

8. Finally, had Haines bought *Raradoa* because he wanted a boat of that type, or because it had been *James Lester's* boat?

We knew that some of these questions were way-out, that we'd let our imaginations rip, that our suspicions could be quite baseless. All the same, with these questions a whole new world of possibilities seemed to have opened up. Noll, who had been very depressed on first hearing about the topaz, suddenly became very active and energetic. Without any more discussion, he had the News Editor and Foreign Editor in and arranged the deployment of our available sleuths for a second round of reports. What we wanted now, he said, in addition to answers to specific questions, was a complete rundown on Haines. And we wanted it fast.

9 P.M.

The reporters are all set to start their new probe—some are already on their way. Paul Briscoe, of the Foreign Room, is on a night flight to Geneva, en route for Chamonix. Edith Curtis has started a telephone check with Shirley's employers about her Continental schedule. Willie Frost is covering the Haines end at Walton. By midday tomorrow we should have a pretty complete dossier.

Meanwhile, our enemies are going to have a field day over the topaz.

22

SOURCE. B.B.C. Television News. Wednesday, April 18th. 10 P.M.
Extract.

". . . This discovery, which was made in the presence of a large number of reporters and of the new owner of the boat, is the most sensational turn yet in the developing Lester drama.

"Mr. Lester himself has not been available for comment since the finding of the topaz. He was to have appeared tonight at Saint Pancras

74

Town Hall, where he had been billed to speak, but the chairman announced that he had become indisposed at the last moment, and Mr. Leslie Shirman deputized for him. At the moment there is some uncertainty about Mr. Lester's whereabouts.

"Miss Shirley Holt told our reporter this evening, 'I'm very pleased that my topaz has been found—I didn't really expect to see it again. I'm writing to Mr. Haines to apologize for the trouble I've caused him.' "

23

SOURCE. Editorial comment in the London *Globe*. Morning of Thursday, April 19th.

The time has come to speak out.

Mr. James Lester has failed to explain to the public how the topaz discovered yesterday in the boat he formerly owned came to be there. Miss Holt says she lost it when she spent a night with him on the boat last autumn. Mr. Lester says nothing. Even his whereabouts is now unknown. Last night he was stated to be indisposed. Is he genuinely ill? Or has he gone into hiding from the press and the voters?

The public are rapidly forming their own judgment about Mr. Lester, and it is an increasingly unfavorable one. As our latest public opinion poll shows, the squalid revelations of recent days have brought about a dramatic change in the fortunes of the parties. From being nearly 25 percentage points in the lead a week ago, the Progressives are now a mere 7 points ahead. This slump in their support seems certain to continue as fresh discoveries throw ever greater doubt on Mr. Lester's veracity and integrity.

A General Election which should have been fought on great national issues, issues of political principle, is now in danger of being decided on an irrelevant matter of personal behavior. Britain is becoming divided as France was once divided by the Dreyfus case. Anger is rising. Families are split. The sordid drama of the Lester affair is doing great harm to Britain. The time has come to end it.

For the sake of his country and of his party, the tarnished leader of the Progressives should withdraw from the political scene before even greater damage is done.

24

SOURCE. Linda Tandy's diary. Thursday, April 19th.

Well, it was to be expected. Not only the *Globe* but most of the press was hostile to James this morning. How could it be anything else, on the evidence? And without a word from him. The political correspondents are writing for the first time of a possible crisis of leadership in the Progressive Party. Our own postbag at the office this morning is bulging with criticism and abuse of James. Fleet Street is buzzing with rumors —that James has been assaulted in Smith Square by an angry crowd, that a letter bomb has been intercepted at the House, that he's had a breakdown and gone into a nursing home, that the party executive is meeting to consider the position. His HQ was tight-lipped—they wouldn't say where he was or even if they knew. All they'd say was that he wouldn't be speaking at his scheduled meeting tonight—the second cancellation. Noll tried hard to break through the barrier, but got the brush-off like everyone else.

Naturally, we're both terribly worried. James was obviously under strain when he telephoned yesterday evening. He must have changed his mind about attending the Saint Pancras meeting almost as he put the phone down. Where did he go and what is he doing? I do hope we'll hear from him soon.

Meanwhile, our Haines probe goes on. The first reports should be coming in in an hour or two.

25

SOURCE. Report to the *Post* by Paul Briscoe, telephoned from Chamonix, France. Thursday, April 19th. 11 A.M.

This is a preliminary report, for urgent attention.

I reached Geneva in the early hours, picked up the hire car, and drove through the mountains (what a road!) to Chamonix and the Bellevue Hotel, where I snatched a little sleep. At eight this morning I started to telephone around to find out where Haines had stayed in January. There are dozens of hotels and pensions here, but I assumed that a well-heeled man on his own would have gone for something pretty comfortable, so I started at the top and worked down. I traced him at the third call. He had a single room with private bath at the Bonheur from January 10th to January 20th.

I drove to the Bonheur to make more inquiries. They remembered him well because of his broken leg. (That's one question answered. I'll try to see the doctor later for details.) Apart from that, almost the first thing I learned (from one of the porters) was that until his accident

Haines had gone skiing every morning with a very attractive blond girl, about twenty-five years old and not French.

I thought you'd like to have this item right away.

26

SOURCE. Report to the *Post* by William Frost on his inquiries at Walton. Thursday, April 19th. Noon.

I had a long talk with Haines and Mrs. Haines early today. I told them what Jim Lester had said, that the topaz must have been planted at some time, and that we were concerned to find out if and when and how it could have been done. Haines was a bit skeptical about the planting in general, and certain it couldn't have been done while the boat was in his possession, but he was interested in the possibilities and quite ready to discuss them. So we started by going over all the basic dates and facts about the purchase and delivery of the boat to see if there were any loopholes. Following is a summary:

The boat was advertised for sale in the *Telegraph* (possibly in other papers, too, but that was where H. saw the ad) on December 27th, as the property of James Lester, M.P. Haines was particularly interested because he had wanted to buy a secondhand boat of this type for some time. Apparently *Raradoa* is a Beacon 27, a very successful design, built by Ruffs of Gosport. Not many of the design reach the secondhand market, and Haines had in fact advertised for one himself last spring in the *Yachting Gazette*, without success. (This answers one of your specific questions. I'll check with the *Y.G.* later that the ad went in, but I've no doubt it did.) Anyway, Haines wrote off at once, and Lester telephoned him, and they made arrangements for an inspection. They met at the Blackwater marina, with Haines's surveyor, on January 4th. (Incidentally Haines says he took to Lester—thought him a splendid chap.) The boat had been hauled out, so the survey didn't take long. As you know, it was satisfactory and the deal was completed. The boat was left locked, and the three men departed at the same time in their respective cars.

Haines told me he didn't return to the boat before it was delivered to his home. I checked this by telephone with the marina. They said that *Raradoa* had been berthed very close to the office, and that if Haines or anyone else had entered the boat he would undoubtedly have been seen by one of the watchmen. The only people to approach *Raradoa* after the sale had been the men from the delivery firm on the day it was removed.

I asked Haines what had happened about Lester's belongings, and he said Lester had taken everything out before they met—so in fact he *didn't* see the contents. We can check this with Lester—though it must be true.

To continue. On January 8th Haines got in touch with East & Co., a Walton firm, and arranged with them that they should collect the boat from the Blackwater marina and deliver it by road to the garden of his Walton home, together with a tarpaulin and the necessary ropes for laying up. He himself would provide the balks of timber for it to stand on and have the site prepared, which he did. The actual delivery was to take place after his return from his skiing trip. On January 10th he flew to France, and on January 20th he returned with his leg in plaster. The boat was delivered and snugged down by the contractors on January 22nd, under Haines's watchful if rather rueful eye.

During all this period, from Haines's receipt of the keys to the date of delivery, the cabin was locked up, and according to Haines it has been locked ever since. Haines had the two keys on his key ring all the time, both in England and in Chamonix. At no time, he says, did he part with them to anyone.

79

I asked Haines if he'd been in residence at his home through the whole period since the delivery of the boat. He said yes, apart from one night in February, which he'd spent in the hospital after the removal of a splinter of bone from his leg—but his wife had been at home that night, and anyway, if I was thinking of a possible intruder, there'd still have been the problem of the keys.

I also asked him if he could remember what the weather had been like around the time the boat had been delivered. He said he could remember very well, because he'd remarked to his wife at the time how fortunate they'd been. The morning of the delivery day had been dry, but the contractors had barely got the boat lashed down under its tarpaulin when heavy rain had started, which had gone on all night. It was that rain, Haines said, which must have filled the pool in the tarpaulin, because there'd been nothing comparable afterward. He reckoned the outer concentric ring on the canvas, which he'd seen in photographs, had been fixed that night.

I checked the weather pattern for January 22nd with the Meteorological Office later, and they confirmed the heavy overnight rain in Essex for that date.

Finally, a word about the Haineses' husband-wife relationship. Mrs. H., though very fat, is by no means unattractive. The couple appear devoted to each other, and jointly to their daughters Julia and Anne. The solo Chamonix trip was actually suggested by Mrs. H., who felt her husband wasn't getting enough of the vigorous exercise he enjoyed. This was the first time he had ever been on holiday without her—and Haines says it will probably be the last!

27

SOURCE. Report to the *Post* by Edith Curtis on Shirley Holt's
Continental movements. Thursday, April 19th.

Using the list that Willie Frost got from Shirley, I finally managed to reach all the British employers by telephone. Their reactions to my inquiries varied, but in the end they all gave me the information I wanted. The Foreign Room had some difficulty over Mme. Laporte, who has moved to Nice, but they finally tracked her down.

Briefly, the situation is this. All the facts and dates that Shirley Holt gave to Willie are confirmed. From the time she was picked up by the Devereux family on September 10th and taken to Saint-Jean-de-Luz, until she left Menton on April 9th, she was on the Continent without a break. Her confirmed schedule was so tight that it would have been impossible for her even to fly back to the U.K. between jobs and still keep her appointments as she did.

The Foreign Room has checked with the hotel where she said she stayed in Paris, and they confirm that she was there for the nights of April 9th, 10th, and 11th, and left late on the 12th to catch the night ferry.

In short, Shirley left the U.K. on September 10th and didn't get back here until April 13th.

Additional note

It occurred to me that while we were making these inquiries it would be worth asking if any of the employers remembered seeing Shirley wearing her topaz ring, since in that case her story of losing the topaz on the boat would be disproved. Alas! The only people who did remember the ring were the Tancreds, and that was before the alleged night on the boat. Another point, I fear, for Shirley.

28

SOURCE. Second report to the *Post* by Paul Briscoe, telephoned from Chamonix. Thursday, April 19th.

I'm sorry to say I misled you badly with my early flash. Too much zeal! My profound apologies.

I've since learned that the attractive blonde Haines was seen with so much was a Norwegian ski instructress temporarily attached to the Chamonix Ski School. Haines, a novice, engaged her through the school to give him instruction for four days, and she called for him at his hotel each morning and took him to the nursery slopes. On the fifth day he went out on his own, tried something too ambitious, and came a cropper.

I found out which hospital he was taken to, and talked to a Dr. Collette, who set his leg. Like doctors everywhere, he was reluctant to say much about a patient, but he confirmed that Haines had sustained a bad double fracture which would require at least one later operation.

When I asked him if he thought that Haines, with his leg in plaster up to the thigh, could have climbed an eight-foot ladder to a boat's cockpit, Collette looked at me in astonishment. He said that a man with unusually strong arms might manage to struggle up such a ladder if it was a matter of life and death, but he couldn't imagine it being attempted in any other circumstances. He said a man who'd badly fractured a leg and splintered some bone would be a very shaken and rather ill man for quite a while, probably in pain and certainly very conscious of the leg. The very last thing he'd think of attempting would be acrobatics on a ladder.

29

SOURCE. Linda Tandy's diary. Thursday, April 19th.

2 P.M.

The Haines reports are all in, and Noll and I have been gloomily contemplating the results of the inquiry. I almost wish now we'd never started it.

This is the picture that has finally emerged about the planting of the topaz:

1. It wasn't planted while James owned the boat, because the cabin was always kept locked and he had the keys. So if it was planted at all it was under Haines's ownership. But not before the delivery of the boat to his home, because no one had visited it at the marina after the sale. And not otherwise than immediately after the rains (query even this) or the concentric mark on the canvas would have been blurred.

2. Haines didn't plant it. It's impossible to believe that a man in his physical condition could have climbed the ladder, balanced on the side deck, hauled up the tarpaulin, folded it back, and got into the cockpit —and later done the whole thing in reverse—all on one leg, with his crutches on the ground. It just isn't on.

3. Mrs. Haines didn't plant it. I've seen pictures of her in the papers, and she's massive. No one of her avoirdupois could have done what was necessary.

4. Shirley didn't plant it. The only relevant time she was in England was April 13th and after, and if the tarpaulin had been disturbed as late as that the pool couldn't possibly have looked as it did.

5. No one could have planted it without the Haineses' knowledge. They've been around all the time, and Haines has had the keys.

So we're left with two possibilities. One is that Haines and his wife are lying, and that someone else planted it *with* their knowledge immediately after the delivery of the boat. But there isn't an iota of evidence to suggest it. As far as the known facts are concerned, they are totally in the clear and totally uninvolved and it would be clutching at straws to think anything else.

The alternative is that the topaz *wasn't* planted.

I was still trying to find a way out of the grim logic of all this, and not succeeding, when Noll suddenly said, "I suppose Jim *is* telling the truth?"

I said, "Oh, *Noll!*" Just to ask the question, openly like that, seemed a betrayal. The possibility that James—James, of all people in the world, James whom I admired so much, so very very much— could have lied and lied was more than I could bear. Yet absolute trust was becoming harder every day, because almost all the evidence was against him. We'd made up our minds from the start that Shirley's story wasn't true, but only because we knew James, not because her story was inherently unbelievable. If any other man had been involved, we almost certainly would have believed her. She'd been consistent, frank, totally undemanding, totally without a motive for lying. Not a flaw had been found by anyone in anything she'd said.

There are questions in my mind today which, even with Noll, I wouldn't wish to put into words. How well do we *really* know James? He and Noll have always been very close, particularly in the last few years, when they've shared the sorrow of having lost people they loved. And I'd certainly have said I knew him well—heaven knows I've studied him enough! But how well can you really know *anyone?* There must always be hidden depths, I suppose, that even a lifetime's association may not uncover. The secret thoughts, the tortuous workings of the private mind—particularly of the subtle and clever mind. Love isn't an X-ray. How great is James's political ambition, how strong his drive for power? How much would he sacrifice of honor to safeguard his career? What effect has the awful tragedy of Mary's death had on him? How have the years of brooding loneliness affected him? Could it possibly be he, rather than Shirley, who is suffering from some deep disturbance of the mind?

I don't know the answers to any of the questions. I only know I want to cry.

Oh, God, what a dreadful day!

30

SOURCE. News paragraph in the London *Star*, midday edition.
Thursday, April 19th.

JIM LESTER MYSTERY

The mystery of Mr. James Lester's whereabouts continues to deepen. He has not been seen or heard from since yesterday evening, when he telephoned his party headquarters saying he was indisposed and would not be appearing at a meeting at Saint Pancras Town Hall, or at another scheduled meeting tonight.

His press secretary today admitted that he had no idea where Mr. Lester was or what he was doing.

It is now known that Mr. Lester did not return to his London flat last night, nor has he been seen at his club. His brother-in-law, Mr. John Fryer, who lives in Brighton, said today that he and his wife had heard nothing.

As a result of Miss Holt's allegations and the public doubts which have been expressed about his personal integrity, Mr. Lester has clearly been under great strain during the past few days. His disappearance is beginning to cause anxiety, and fears are being expressed that he may have come to some harm.

31

SOURCE. Linda Tandy's diary. Friday, April 20th. 1:30 A.M.

The day that began so dreadfully (it's actually "yesterday" now, though it still seems like "today" to me) has ended with some most unexpected and exciting developments. I'm feeling a bit battered, one way and another, but I want to get everything down while it's still in my mind.

That piece in the *Star* had me worried to death, particularly after what I'd been thinking about James's possible mental state. I couldn't really imagine him throwing himself over a cliff or anything like that—the James I felt I knew was much more the man who'd said, "Why flap over a minor personal incident?"—but he'd gone through so much since then it didn't seem absolutely impossible. Particularly when the suggestion was in front of one in cold print, which makes anything seem more likely, even if you know it's merely the result of some journalist turning out a "think piece." And, quite apart from that, there was the fear that he might have become seriously ill somewhere, or had an accident. Anyway, it was ghastly not knowing what had happened to him and I really was in quite a state.

Then, around four in the afternoon, he walked into the office. Just walked in! He came straight up to Noll's room, where I was taking some letters. It was such a relief to see him I could have swooned!

His manner was extraordinary—very concentrated, yet somehow detached. Either he didn't realize (I thought then) how much worse everything had got since the discovery of the topaz—or else, for some reason, he didn't care.

Noll said, "Jim! Where the heck have you been? We've practically been having heart attacks about you."

James looked surprised. "Oh? Why?"

"Haven't you seen the *Star?*"

"No," he said.

Noll passed him our copy, and he read the paragraph with some concern. "Oh, dear!" he said. "I am sorry. It never occurred to me you'd be worrying."

"You *have* been missing for nearly twenty-four hours," Noll said reproachfully.

"I haven't been missing—I've just been busy. Very busy. And preoccupied. There was something I had to find out. . . . Noll, if it's all right with you, I'd like to borrow your daughter for the night."

I let out a giggle, which even in my own ears sounded wildly hysterical. (End of anxiety, start of reaction?) "He'll want at least two camels and three cows for me," I said.

James gave a wintry sort of smile. "Well, let's say for part of the night."

Noll regarded him doubtfully. "What *are* you up to, Jim?"

"I'd sooner not tell you now," James said. "Call it superstition, if you like. . . . It's something I have to try out, that's all. There's nothing very secret about it, but it may not work."

Noll said, "Okay—I won't press you. . . . But—nothing rash, or dangerous, I hope."

"With Linda? Good God, no. It's just a little experiment—quite legal and quite safe. . . . What do you say, Linda?"

I said, "Of course I'll come with you, James." I still felt as though I'd just drunk three martinis on an empty stomach. "What do I need—nightie and toothbrush? Or what?"

"Nothing at all." He looked me up and down, which didn't take long because there's not really much of me. "You're perfect as you are." He said it quite seriously, not jokingly. It was only later that I realized why.

"Where are we going?" I asked him.

"Walton-on-the-Naze," he said. "I'll pick you up in Hampstead at eight o'clock. All right? Now I must rush—I've got some shopping to do. I wonder—would you be very kind, Linda, and give Nancy a ring? [Nancy Fryer, Lester's sister in Brighton. *Ed.*] Tell her I'm fine?"

"Of course," I said.

He turned at the door. "I *should* have telephoned you. Forgive me." He gave a little wave and hurried out. He hadn't asked us what we'd been doing, or given us a chance to tell him. He hadn't even mentioned the topaz.

Noll looked at me a bit blankly after he'd gone. "I hope he's—*all right,*" he said.

James called for me on the dot of eight, and we set off for Walton in his Rover. He said he hadn't been back to HQ—he'd done his shopping and then dropped into a pub for a snack. He asked me if I'd eaten and I said I had. He didn't volunteer anything about the purpose of the journey, but he did say, "This is the second time I've done this trip in twenty-four hours."

I said, "So that's where you were last night."

"Yes. I was doing a bit of reconnaissance."

"At Haines's place?"

"Yes. I wanted to have a look round there after dark."

"We've been making inquiries about Haines," I said. "We don't think he was concerned with any planting."

"I'm sure he wasn't. I had a long talk with him this morning. I like him. *And* his wife."

"Our man talked to him this morning, too. Willie Frost."

"Ah. Then it must have been his car that was leaving when I arrived."

"Where did you spend the night?"

"The Blue Boar at Walton. I was 'L. James' from London."

"I'm surprised no one recognized you."

"I wore dark glasses. I've been living in them. In the short term, they're an excellent protection."

"When are you going to tell me what our trip's all about?"

"When we get to Walton," he said. "It's rather complicated."

He negotiated a roundabout carefully. Then he said, "It must have been difficult for you and Noll to go on believing in me—after what's happened."

"Not really," I said, lying. "We have faith in you. You know that."

"Mmm. Some cynic said that faith is believing something you know to be untrue."

"I'm not a cynic."

"Anyway," he said, "I'm deeply grateful."

He became silent, concentrating on his driving on the busy North Circular. That suited me. I was enjoying the feeling of being in his car, alone with him, which hadn't happened very often before. For some reason, I felt more relaxed than I'd been for days, and at some point I even dozed a little. I must have done, because I can remember hardly anything of the journey until we were well out into Essex.

James was driving very slowly, hardly more than thirty miles an hour, when I started to take an interest again. I said, "You don't seem to be in a great hurry about anything. What's our deadline?"

He accelerated to normal speed. "There's no deadline. I was thinking."

"About the case?"

"No . . . About Mary, as a matter of fact."

I said, "Oh . . . Sorry I interrupted you."

He was silent for a moment. Then he said, "It was a horrible crash. Did you ever hear the details?"

"I may have done, James—but if so I've forgotten. The details never seemed to matter."

"It was at a crossroads," he said. "An unmarked one. I caught just a glimpse of the other car, just for a second. Then it hit us, and our car seemed to disintegrate. All I could see were bits and pieces scattered about, and Mary lying on the ground. She was groaning. It was awful.

Really awful. No one ever imagines a scene like that—until it happens. Then it's unbelievable. And too late."

I said, "Aren't you being rather morbid—dwelling on it now?"

"I'm not really dwelling on it—I'm just recalling. She was in hospital for a month, you know. I went to see her every day, but she had only one moment of lucidity. I'd taken some flowers—the way one does, hopefully. She opened her eyes, and I showed her the flowers. Do you know what she said? She said, 'They'll do to put on my grave.' I wouldn't have thought that anyone ever actually said a thing like that. But she said it. And five days later she died."

I gave a little murmur of sympathy. I couldn't think of anything useful to say, especially as it had all happened so long ago. I couldn't see why he wanted to talk about it. It seemed extraordinary, when he had so much else on his mind.

There was another pause. Then he said, "It was my fault, you know. I was driving much too fast. Thinking about something else—not paying attention. It was my fault she died."

I said, "Everybody drives too fast sometimes. No one *always* pays proper attention. You really mustn't go on blaming yourself."

"No," he said. "That would be stupid. . . . But I wanted to get it off my chest. I wanted you to know, that's all." He seemed to stress the *you.*

He said no more about it, and presently he began to hum softly in the darkness. It was as though he had exorcised a ghost.

We reached Walton just before eleven o'clock. It was pretty quiet, with little traffic about. James threaded his way knowledgeably through some side streets and finally pulled up outside a biggish house in a leafy suburban road. "This is Haines's place," he said. He switched off the engine. "You can't see from here, but a few yards along the road to the left there's a footpath, a public right-of-way, that runs along the outside of his garden wall. There's a wrought-iron gate in the wall, opening into the garden. It has a latch, but no lock. The boat is quite near the gate, on the right as you go in." He reached into the back of the car, brought up a canvas bag, and took some things out, which he passed to me. One was a three-foot length of rubber tubing. One was a three-foot length of round, flexible plastic rod. One was a thin pencil torch. "Now this is what I want you to try and do," he said—and he gave me some very precise instructions. At last I knew the purpose of the journey.

I looked up at the house. Most of it was in darkness, but I could see a faint light in a window facing the side where the boat was, and not all that far away from it. I said, "What do I do if someone raises the alarm?"

"No one will," James said. "I've fixed it with Haines. He'll be watching and listening, so it's important to be as quiet as possible. With luck he'll neither see nor hear you. If he does, he'll merely tell me afterward. There's no dog, by the way. Good luck!"

I waited a moment to let a passing car get clear. Then I walked quickly along the road to the path, my heart thumping. There might be no danger, but I felt that an awful lot depended on me. I found the wrought-iron gate, opened it with only the tiniest squeak, and slipped into the garden. I could see the boat towering up on the right, a looming shape against the starlit sky. I crept along the inside of the wall and squeezed myself into the narrow space between the wall and the boat's hull. I could see now why James had needed me. No man bigger than a dwarf could have operated there.

I switched on the pencil torch and ran the tiny beam along the hull, identifying one by one the several outlets that James had told me about. His description had been very exact, and I soon found the one that mattered. I worked my way a little farther along till I had it directly in line. It was slightly past the center of the hull, well below the painted waterline, but above my head. I struggled up onto one of the balks of timber and somehow got my arms up past my body without letting go of the vital gear. I made sure which end of the rubber tube had James's new topaz wedged in it, and pushed the tube up into the outlet pipe till it wouldn't go any farther. Then I poked the round plastic rod into the tube and pushed that, too. There was a little resistance at first, but when I pushed harder, easing the tube a little, it suddenly ended—and there was a faint clink as the stone dropped. I pulled the rod and tube out together, climbed down from the timber balk, worked my way out past the hull and along the wall to the gate, and hurried back to the car. The whole thing had taken less than five minutes. The tiny torch beam had been obscured from the house by the hull, and I'd hardly made a sound.

"I think it worked," I said as I collapsed rather breathlessly into the passenger seat. "In fact, I'm sure it did. . . . It was a marvelous idea, James. How did you come to think of it?"

"A simple matter of elimination," James said. "No other way seemed possible." He took my hand and gently squeezed it. "Thanks, Linda. Thanks for everything. I don't know what I'd do without you." Then he leaned over and kissed me, his arms around me.

I was suddenly back with those three martinis. Head spinning, blood surging. When he released me—which wasn't for quite a time—I said shakily, "That'll cost you another camel!"

He murmured something quite ridiculous—about it being "just an avuncular kiss."

If any uncle of mine had kissed me like that, I'd have avoided him forevermore!

32

SOURCE. Report of a press conference held by James Lester, M.P.,
at Progressive Party HQ on Friday, April 20th, at 11 A.M.
Extract.

"Good morning, ladies and gentlemen. As you can see, I haven't fallen
under a bus, as some of you feared—or hoped. (*Scattered laughter*.) I
have merely been rather occupied.

"Before we come to your questions, I have an item of information
which I think may interest you. Yesterday morning, most if not all of
your papers splashed the story of Miss Holt's topaz being found in the
boat I used to own, and most of you drew the conclusion that Miss Holt
must have been with me on the boat as she says, since on the evidence
there was no other way the topaz could have got there.

"I now invite you to return to the boat—I have the permission of Mr.
Haines, the new owner, for this—where you will find another topaz in
the place where the first one was found. Mr. Haines will tell you that
no one has re-entered the boat since it was closed up by newsmen the
day before yesterday, and that at no time has he seen or heard anything
indicating an approach to the boat, although he has been keeping a
special lookout. As I was responsible for the planting of this second
stone, perhaps one of you would be kind enough to retrieve it for me
when you have finished your investigations. Like the original, it is of no
great value, but it may have some slight historical interest one day! You
will have to work out for yourselves how the introduction was effected,
but I can tell you it was a very simple matter and took only a few

minutes. It will be apparent to you, I'm sure, that if I could plant the second stone without detection, someone else could have planted the first one just as easily by the same method.

"Now perhaps we could turn to more serious matters. . . ."

33

SOURCE. Linda Tandy's diary. Friday, April 20th.

4 P.M.

Today started quite promisingly—at least in comparison with the gloom of recent days. The reporters at the press conference positively stampeded for their cars after James's statement and rushed down to Walton to check. Haines—what a nice man! How could we ever have suspected him?—was waiting for them with the cabin keys and a big grin. They opened up the boat again and found the topaz in the U-bend —so our efforts last night had worked as we thought they had. No one doubted the assurances of Haines and Mrs. Haines that the boat had not been re-entered since the first inspection. So by lunchtime things had begun to look much better, and Noll and I were almost cheerful. We were even getting some amusement from James's studied pretense that the whole case is just a frivolous diversion from matters of importance. Unfortunately, the euphoria hasn't lasted.

The evening papers are still skeptical and hostile. One of them head-lined its report of the new discovery "HOUDINI LESTER WINS A TRICK." The view is that while James has shown, by some clever piece of magic-circle business, that the first topaz *could* have been planted in the boat, he has by no means proved that it *was*. The first stone, they say, could well have been the result of a genuine loss by Miss Holt, and only the second one planted. The impression they give is that James has been too clever by half. If the public goes along with this—and it's in the mood for it—James and I will have achieved very little, if anything, by our trip to Walton.

There's been no response so far to any of the advertisements asking the owner of the Sound of Mull motor cruiser to get in touch. Considering the worldwide publicity that vessel has had, it's hard to believe that someone aboard wouldn't have heard of the appeal by now. It looks as though we were right: they just don't want to come forward. Even though James did take the navigational blame to encourage them. If this is what they call the camaraderie of the sea, I don't think much of it!

7 P.M.

Another awful shock tonight. Very bad news from Scotland—the worst blow yet. We no sooner struggle to our feet than we're knocked flat again. . . .

34

SOURCE. Telephoned report by Andrew Macdonald, stringman for the *Post* in Oban. Friday, April 20th.

Following reports of some sensational gossip in local pubs, I and other newsmen today interviewed two fishermen of good repute and standing in Oban—Charles McNeill and David Bruce, who jointly own and run the motor fishing vessel *Jeannie*.

They said that they'd been following the Lester case, dates and so on, and had now worked things out, and they thought they should say what they knew. They said that on the afternoon of September 5th last they were returning to Oban, after a sea trip, with a particularly good catch, and were talking of having a booze-up to celebrate, because it was also David's birthday. They said they were passing the north coast of Mull sometime in the afternoon—they can't remember exactly when— steaming quite close to the land and just to seaward of an anchored yacht which they now realized must have been Lester's. There was no sign of anyone on board, but there were two people lying side by side on the beach of a little cove opposite—a man and a woman—and they were naked. Just for fun, McNeill fetched a camera from below and took a photograph of them.

I have seen the photograph. The figures are certainly of a man and a woman, but the detail is not clear enough to show their features.

I asked McNeill and Bruce if they had noticed whether there was a dinghy either tied up to the yacht or beached ashore. They said they hadn't noticed. I imagine they were too busy noticing the nudes! We don't get much of that up here. On beaches, I mean.

They are both sturdily independent men and reliable characters, quite incapable of inventing such a story and faking a photograph. I think their evidence, as far as it goes, undoubtedly has to be accepted.

35

SOURCE. Editorial in the *Star*. Morning of Saturday, April 21st.

LESTER MUST GO

The independent testimony of the two Oban fishermen, Mr. McNeill and Mr. Bruce, which we print on another page, must surely put an end to speculation about who is lying and who is not in the sordid Lester affair. The weight of evidence is now overwhelming.

Let us briefly review that evidence.

Miss Holt says she met Mr. Lester on a Scottish beach on September 5th last. Mr. Lester admits that he was in his boat close by that beach on that day.

Miss Holt says Mr. Lester sunbathed with her in the nude on the beach. The two fishermen say they *saw* a man and a woman sunbathing nude on the beach, and they have a photograph to prove it.

Miss Holt says she spent the night on Mr. Lester's boat. Mr. Lester says he was sailing alone in the Sound of Mull. But he has failed to produce any witnesses. A vessel which he says passed close to him has conspicuously failed to materialize in spite of worldwide efforts to trace it.

Miss Holt has described Mr. Lester's boat and its contents in the greatest detail. Mr. Lester has been unable to explain how she could have done so had her story not been true.

Miss Holt says she lost a topaz on the boat. A topaz has been found on the boat. Mr. Lester says it was planted. He has demonstrated that it *could* have been. But he is silent about who might have done it. Why? Because a vague charge is hard to rebut? And a specific one might be disproved?

There is a well-known Latin tag—*Cui bono?*—much used by lawyers. It means, "Who benefits?" Miss Holt has certainly not benefited from her disclosures—rather the reverse. But Mr. Lester has benefited—so far —by his denials. He still has his seat in the House of Commons, his Shadow Cabinet job, his political hopes.

In the light of all the evidence now available, including the evidence of the fishermen, we venture to say that if this matter came before a court today there is not a jury in the land that would not find for Miss Holt and against Mr. Lester.

We repeat what we said three days ago. Mr. Lester is discredited. He can no longer be regarded as a credible alternative Prime Minister. He should resign his party leadership now, and remove himself from the public scene.

36

SOURCE. Linda Tandy's diary. Saturday, April 21st.

All the papers are terrible this morning—the *Star* the worst, but only marginally. I gave them a quick glance and then couldn't bear to read any more. I'm feeling punch-drunk and hardly capable of rational thought. After Macdonald's report, there seems no case for the defense at all—unless the fishermen are in on some act, which is *most* unlikely. I'm plunged back into the deepest depression. I don't know what the answer is—if there is an answer. Noll sent James a carbon of Macdonald's message, and of course he'll have read this morning's press, but he's said nothing, except that he wasn't the man on the beach. Probably he doesn't know what to say, any more than the rest of us. Probably he's thinking things over. He's never been one to *rush* into speech or print. And he must have so much on his mind besides this personal battle. An election campaign can't be anything but an enormous strain—even when everything goes smoothly. When almost everyone is baying for your blood, it must be hell.

The mood of the country is getting very ugly. Our postbag is quite obscene—and *our* readers are supposed to be James's supporters. Things can't go on like this.

Noll lunched today with Craven, who, as chairman of the parliamentary party, was naturally sunk in gloom. He'd just had a preview of the latest poll figures, which he said were shattering—a big percentage lead for the government. He now saw only two possibilities. If the Progressives sacked James and chose a new leader—which would be the second change in a matter of weeks—they'd regain some ground but would be beaten. If they kept James, they'd be overwhelmed, and would end up as a tiny rump, like the Labour Party in 1931. A decision would have to be taken in the next two or three days at latest. He thought James would probably resign when the crunch came, rather than split his party irremediably. Noll said he still thought the evidence quite inconclusive, and that some very peculiar things were happening. Craven snorted, and said the evidence didn't have to be conclusive with an emotional electorate, which never read much further than the headlines, anyway.

Apparently James has resumed his campaign as though nothing new had happened. We haven't seen or heard anything from him today— he's been completely tied up. Tonight he's addressing a meeting out of town—Chelmsford, I think. He has tremendous guts—but where's it getting him?

I'm lost—quite lost.

37

SOURCE. National Press Agency. On tape to subscribers. Saturday, April 21st.

20:15   FLASH. James Lester injured.

20:25   Lester slightly injured in face by flying object during hostile demonstration at Chelmsford tonight.

100

20:55   Lester full.

Mr. James Lester had to be rescued by police this evening from a hostile crowd, many of them his own former supporters, after a meeting he had begun to address at Chelmsford had been broken up.

The meeting was fairly orderly until Mr. Lester rose to speak. Then dozens of youths erupted at the back of the hall, shouting abuse and obscenities, advancing toward the platform and throwing missiles. Fights broke out in several parts of the hall which the stewards were unable to cope with. Women screamed and tried to reach the exits, and for a time there was a risk of panic. Police were called in, and after reinforcements had arrived and some twenty arrests had been made, a semblance of order was restored.

Mr. Lester, who had sustained a slight cut on the forehead from a flying missile, then attempted to continue his address, but after further noisy demonstrations he conferred with the chairman and the meeting was abandoned.

Police attempted to smuggle Mr. Lester from the hall by a back exit, but a threatening crowd had already gathered there and it took some fifty officers, some of them mounted, to clear a way and escort Mr. Lester safely to his car.

38

SOURCE. Linda Tandy's diary. Saturday. April 21st.

Midnight

Well, there was a really dramatic turn of events this evening—and I don't mean the riot at Chelmsford.

Noll and I got the news about that at the flat when Parker, the Saturday night duty man at the *Post*, rang up shortly before nine. By then, fortunately, it had been confirmed that James's injury was trivial, so we weren't too worried. I mean, not much more than we had been before!

We listened to the ten o'clock news to see if there was anything fresh, which there wasn't, and I'd just switched off when James phoned. He said he was on his way back from Chelmsford and asked if he could call in at the flat and have a talk. Noll said of course, and that we'd heard about his rough meeting, and was he all right, and James said he was.

He arrived half an hour later. Except for a small crisscross of plaster that someone had stuck on his forehead, he didn't look in the least like a man who'd narrowly escaped lynching. In fact, he was rather chipper. He was quite offhand about the meeting—said it was the sort of thing that was only to be expected in the circumstances. He thought perhaps he'd have to cut out his speaking engagements till things were cleared up, since he didn't seem to be doing any good for the party or himself —but he didn't appear too concerned about that. Noll poured him a whisky, but he only took a sip. Something else, I sensed, was keeping

102

him going. I couldn't imagine what, unless he'd thought up some way of getting round the evidence of the Oban fishermen, which seemed unlikely. In fact he didn't mention them—not at first. His concern was with something quite different.

"That list," he said. "That detailed list of things Shirley Holt said she'd seen on the boat."

"What about it?" Noll asked.

"Well," James said, "I gave it hardly more than a glance when you sent it to me. The items all seemed accurate as far as I could remember, and then the topaz business came up and put everything else out of my mind. . . . I thought, as you did, that Shirley couldn't have seen all those things from the quay and that she must have got her information from someone who'd been in the cabin—but there were so many of those that it didn't help. . . . It was only tonight, as I drove back from Chelmsford, that I realized I'd overlooked something important about one of the items. That ship in the bottle—remember?"

"I remember it was on the list," Noll said. "I assumed it must have been right, or you'd have said something. I didn't notice it myself."

"No, you wouldn't have done—because when you were on the boat it wasn't there. You see, I bought that bottle in a Tobermory yacht chandler's on the morning of September 5th, before I sailed out to the anchorage. I thought it would make an amusing present for Teddie. [A young nephew. *Ed.*] I stowed it away in the locker under my bunk for safety, and I had it with me in the boat for a time, and when I left Oban on the sixth, I took it to London with me. Now it's true there were one or two people who might have known or guessed that I had it on board —for instance, the shop assistant who sold it to me—but there was only one person who could have known for certain that it was on board and *in a locker under one of the bunks,* as Shirley said, because from the morning of the fifth until I left the boat in Oban on the sixth, only one person came into the cabin."

It was like the sighting of land after a long voyage of discovery. I said, "Who? The harbor master?"

"No—he was there earlier. . . . It was that yacht deliverer, Frank Jackson. I asked him aboard for a drink before lunch on the morning I returned from my unsuccessful night trip. He was interested in boats of any kind, but particularly in *Raradoa*, as he'd never been aboard a Beacon 27, so I showed him all over it—the accommodation, the cupboards, the washroom, the lockers, the lot. He'd have seen all the things mentioned in Shirley's list, including the bottle—and at some time he must have told her about them."

"You make it sound like a certainty," Noll said.

"It *is* a certainty, Noll. The logic's inescapable. Shirley couldn't have known herself that the bottle was in the locker. Therefore someone told her. Only Jackson knew. Therefore Jackson told her."

"Yes—I can't see any flaw in that. . . . You're quite *sure* no one was aboard except Jackson?"

"Absolutely certain."

"Mmm . . . So Jackson takes the place of our former suspect Haines. It's he, you think, who's in collusion with Shirley."

"I'd say so, yes. There's more evidence—at least, *I* think so—that points the same way."

"What's that?"

"The report of the Oban fishermen. Obviously one has to accept their testimony as true and genuine. So it's now clear that there *were* two people lying nude on the beach that afternoon. Of course, practically everyone has decided that I was one of them—but *I* know I wasn't. So who were they? And what led Shirley to use two nude sunbathers in her story? What gave her the notion? You could say, perhaps, that they could have been any two people—that Shirley had just happened to spot them when she was out for a walk on the cliffs. But would she have dared to tell the world she was sunbathing there with me if she'd known there'd been two other people in the cove that afternoon, two strangers, who might at some time have come forward and given evidence about the strange coincidence? I very much doubt it. I suggest that Shirley thought of the nude-sunbathing episode, and felt safe in using it, because she was one of the sunbathers and the other was her fellow conspirator—and probably her boyfriend—Frank Jackson."

I thought it was a most impressive reconstruction—and typical of James's clear thinking. (He'd have made a devastating counsel. If only he'd stuck to the bar!) I particularly went for the last bit, about Jackson being Shirley's boyfriend. It had seemed odd from the beginning that a girl as attractive as Shirley should have been going around at the age of twenty-six without a hint of a male in sight—as though there was no such thing as love or sex in the world. It just wasn't natural. My spirits, which for days had been registering highs and lows like some crazy barometer, suddenly soared again. Perhaps, at last, we were getting somewhere. All the same, I could see several snags in the theory—and so could Noll.

"You aren't forgetting, are you," I said, "that Jackson is about the only man in the country who's said anything useful on your behalf? His comments on that drooping flag business—remember? He needn't have said what he did. *And* he allowed himself to be quoted. He was scathing about Shirley, too; he said some very rough things about her to John Fletcher. He seemed to be all on your side."

"He did seem to be," James agreed. "But perhaps he knew there'd be enough evidence on the other side to outweigh anything he said. In that case, he was being rather clever—fending off any possible suspicion of himself, without doing me any permanent good."

"Ye-es," Noll said. "All right, we'll let that go. But this idea of yours that he could have been with Shirley on the beach . . . I seem to remember that Jackson was at the harbor around five that afternoon, shifting his boat to a new berth. That's what the harbor master told our man."

"I know—but he could still have been with Shirley earlier in the afternoon. The walk back to Tobermory would have taken him less than an hour. He could have left her on the beach. In fact, come to think of it, he must have done."

"You're ahead of me," Noll said. "Why do you say 'must'?"

"Because somebody must have known I was anchored there on my own pretty well till dusk—otherwise Shirley's story would have been too risky. I might have cleared off and been spotted by someone else, in daylight, miles away. So I'm sure one of them was on the beach, or at least within sight of me, till quite late—and it could only have been Shirley. That probably suited them, anyway: they obviously wouldn't have wanted to leave together. If you're on conspiring terms with a man, you don't show yourself publicly with him if you can help it. I see their meeting as a pretty hush-hush affair."

"That would go with Shirley staying at the motel," I said. "We know it's an easy place to slip in and out of without being noticed. Perhaps that's why she chose it. Perhaps there were other discreet meetings while she was on her own at Tobermory."

We were silent for a while, thinking about it. Then Noll said, "How about the topaz, Jim? How would you fit Jackson into that bit of work?"

"Well," James said, "he couldn't have put the stone into the boat himself, of course—he's far too big. But he could have got Shirley to do it—she's slim enough."

"When could he? She was on the Continent till the thirteenth; we've checked that. And from the fourteenth onward, she had newsmen on her heels all the time."

"She could have put it there the night of the day she got back," James said. "The night of the thirteenth—before there was any interest in her. Jackson could have reconnoitered beforehand, the way I did. He could have picked her up somewhere and taken her to Walton, as I took Linda."

"Mmm—it's possible, I suppose. . . ." Noll reflected. "There are an awful lot of unanswered questions, though, aren't there? Supposing you're right—when did they think up all this business? When did they work out the details? How did they manage to keep in touch, right up to the end? It's not as though it was a simple plot—the staff work would have been enormous. . . . And where would it get them? Where's the motive?"

"I agree about all that," James said. "I know there's a lot we can't explain—*yet*. But I'm sure we're on the right track with Jackson. He has the qualifications—he knew everything that was necessary. He knew I'd been sailing with a companion, and where, and about your recall, because I told him. He knew all about *Raradoa,* because I showed him, and he'd have been observant because he was interested. He knew I planned to leave for Oban on the fifth, because I discussed the trip with him. He knew, next day, that I'd attempted the passage and turned back —and so had no alibi for the night. If he was on the beach, he'd certainly have recognized the boat as it lay offshore. He'd have had no difficulty in discovering the name and address of the new owner, because he'd have seen the boat was registered: the number's carved in a timber. Or of thinking up a way of getting the topaz into the U-bend—with his knowledge of boats it would have been obvious. So many things fit. . . ."

"Well," Noll said after a pause, "it's certainly the most persuasive idea anyone's had yet. . . . All right, let's follow it up. We know almost nothing about Jackson at the moment, except that he's a self-styled yacht deliverer. We'd better do with him what we did with Haines— get to work on him."

James nodded. "I think so. The only thing is, if we're right about him he's going to be very cagey at a second approach, isn't he? Haines wasn't, but then he was in the clear. Jackson's bound to be suspicious."

"Not necessarily," Noll said. "We can say we're keen to do a feature article on yacht delivering. It's an unusual job; it must be full of color and excitement. Packed with interest for our sailing readers! I'll get on to it first thing in the morning."

That's how we left things.

39

SOURCE. Report by John Fletcher on a second interview with Frank
Jackson. Sunday, April 22nd. Reports telephoned to the *Post*
1 P.M. and 4 P.M.

Any doubts about Frank Jackson's readiness to talk were soon dispelled.
He was tickled to death at the idea of a feature article on yacht delivering
in his favorite newspaper, with himself as the central figure, and he
couldn't have been more forthcoming. We started with a general talk
about the job and how it operated. Some of the facts that emerged were
as follows:

1. With the enormous increase in yachting in the past year or two,
there is never any shortage of work. On the contrary, Jackson is constantly having to turn down requests from would-be clients, and he
always has a long list of jobs he's promised to fit in as and when he can.
This is particularly the case in the off-season—October to March. What
happens, he says, is that many yachtsmen make ambitious holiday trips
in the summer, get held up in foreign ports by a run of bad weather,
and have to fly home in order to be back at their jobs on time, leaving
their boats to be collected during the winter months. They always *intend*
to sail them home but can't make it. And as there are comparatively few
reliable deliverers in regular business, compared with the number of jobs,
the pressure is always great.

2. It's a fair living—but depends of course on how many trips you're
prepared to make. The overheads are low for the man operating on his
own; and yachtsmen who go in for lengthy voyages usually have biggish

108

boats and are pretty well-to-do, so the charges can be high. These charges have to cover all travel and personal expenses en route to and from the job, and often the expenses of a crew as well.

3. Jackson has several fishermen buddies he can ask to crew for him when he needs someone. The two he uses most often are Joe Ensor, of Brightlingsea, and Tom Billings, of Tollesbury—both places near here. He never takes more than one man on a passage. Whenever possible—i.e., on short voyages in settled weather or when there are conveniently placed ports or rivers he can put in to for the night—he sails alone, which he prefers. He never attempts to hurry over a job, having a liking for looking around new places, and he always makes this clear to clients from the start. The routine for a collection from abroad with a crew is that Jackson flies out first and gets the boat ready, and the crew joins him when he gives the word—thus saving expense. Conversely, after a delivery abroad the crew flies home and Jackson stays to do the clearing up.

4. Jackson says his personal preference is for less money and quite long intervals ashore between jobs. He says he enjoys the work most of the time, or he wouldn't do it, but it's almost always hard and wearing, and of course in bad weather it can be risky. He told me some hair-raising stories of the condition some yachts were in when he took them over; the owners insist they're well-found, but on inspection they turn out to be old tore-outs, with leaky hulls and worn ropes and neglected engines. If they're too bad, he packs in the job. There's plenty of good copy on all this, if we ever run the feature.

5. I told Jackson I thought our readers would be interested in the actual deliveries he'd made recently—say, in the last six months. He showed me his records and his log and a file of correspondence with satisfied, waiting, and rejected clients. He left me alone with the stuff while he made some phone calls, so there was no problem about copying down the particulars. The names of recent clients are attached, for verification if necessary. The deliveries he has made during the period we are interested in are as follows:

a. Sept. 2–11. Delivery 73. 27-foot sloop *Miranda.* Island of Coll to Clyde. No crew. (In port at Tobermory Sept 3–7 for repair to water pump.)

b. Oct. 9–20. Delivery 74. 45-foot twin screw diesel yacht *Sea Breeze.* San Sebastián to Falmouth. Crew, Joe Ensor.

c. Dec. 5–15. Delivery 75. 30-foot motor sailer *Agnes.* Huelva to Gibraltar. (Held up by engine trouble in Huelva.) Crew, Tom Billings.

d. March 10–20. Delivery 76. 32-foot ketch *Wanderer.* Genoa to Marseilles. Crew, Joe Ensor.

e. April 7–11. Delivery 77. 50-foot motor cruiser *Vent du Sud.* (French client.) Ramsgate to Calais. No crew.

6. There is not the slightest doubt that Jackson is running a genuine business as a yacht deliverer, and has been doing so for the past five years. His present way of life (cheap living, oldish car, etc.) gives the impression that he gets by adequately, but no more. He's obviously content with this.

7. I asked him about his earlier activities, including the time he was in the merchant service. He said he'd started as a young man with the Caribbean Shipping Company, mostly carrying bananas; he'd also served for some years with the New Zealand Transport Line. After that he'd taken a shore job with one of the big Hamble boatyards, Gregg & Sons. While he was there, he'd met a wealthy Brazilian who'd offered him a job skippering a luxury yacht based in Bermuda, which he'd accepted. But he'd packed that in after a short time because, in his own words, he "didn't like taking orders from layabouts." He said he preferred not to mention the name of the Brazilian. The other jobs can probably be checked, if desired, with the companies concerned. I'm sure they're okay, as otherwise he would hardly have given me their names.

8. For what it's worth, here's my personal assessment of Jackson after our second meeting. He's undoubtedly a very tough character. Physically he's formidable. When everything's to his liking, he appears amiable,

but I realized today that he has a rather nasty temper. Someone phoned him about a delivery he'd refused, and evidently said something unpleasant, and Jackson seemed to lose all control of himself: he shouted the most lurid collection of nautical expressions into the phone before slamming it down. (I'd hate to meet him again if he ever discovered the real object of this interview!)

Obviously he's a good organizer. He's shrewd and intelligent, but in a fairly simple way. Primarily he's a man of action, not imagination. He's direct rather than subtle. I can't really see him as the originator of an extremely complex conspiracy with a political background. To me it just doesn't figure. Maybe Shirley would fit that bill—I don't know—but again I wouldn't have thought Jackson would be happy taking instructions from a woman, even one as attractive as Shirley Holt. There may be *something* in our theory, but there's also something missing. Basically, a first-class brain.

9. I'm putting this report through right away, in case you need it for further inquiries. I'll then talk to some of the locals and try and see Joe Ensor and Tom Billings, and I'll come through again this afternoon.

Second report

I've had a couple of most interesting conversations—especially interesting because they reinforce an earlier impression.

I talked first with some oystermen along the front here. I mentioned that I was from the press and that I'd been getting some dope from Frank Jackson for an article on yacht delivering, and thought he was a pretty striking character, and I soon got them talking about him, too. They all had the greatest respect for his skill and knowledge as a seaman, and in general they seemed to think he was quite a good bloke. Then one of them said, with a grin, "As long as you don't get on the wrong side of him." I said I'd guessed that maybe he had a bit of a temper, and they said that was right, and told me a few things. Apparently the rumor around these parts—lacking any solid foundation, as far as I could discover—is that Jackson parted company with his wealthy Brazilian after bashing one of his playboy guests! Which could account for J.'s reluctance to mention the Brazilian's name.

This matter of the violent temper came up again when I talked to Joe Ensor. (Billings is away fishing.) Ensor, like the oystermen, was full of praise for Jackson's skill at his craft, and obviously admired him. He said he'd found him a good companion aboard ship, cool in any emergency, and (oddly enough) quite good-tempered at sea. It was ashore, Ensor said, that you could get into bad trouble with him. He told me that in a Toulon pub, on one occasion, Jackson had severely beaten up a French sailor who'd got across him, and had had to be literally dragged away. "He just sees red," Ensor said.

Incidentally, the impression I got a few days ago that Jackson is a bit of a womanizer with a girl in every port—which arose from a joking remark he made—appears to be quite wrong. Ensor said that, except on one occasion, he'd never known Jackson to bother about women at all while he was on jobs abroad—or, for that matter, at home either. I naturally asked him about the one occasion, and Ensor said it had been a year or so back when he'd joined Jackson at Le Havre to help him bring a yacht back to Portsmouth. J. had been banging about the boat in a diabolical temper, and had muttered something about a girl having let him down and if it happened again he'd bloody well kill her.

In different circumstances, I'd think this uncontrolled aspect of Jackson's character illuminating. If we were investigating a brutal murder, for instance, with J. under suspicion, his erratically violent nature would obviously be important. But in the present case, where the emphasis is on subtlety and cunning, with no element of violence at all, it seems irrelevant.

40

SOURCE. Linda Tandy's diary. Sunday, April 22nd.

John Fletcher's report from West Mersea has moved things on quite a bit. Even Noll, a doubter to start with, is now ready to believe we may be on the right track with Jackson.

The report didn't strike us as very helpful at first reading. Jackson seemed confirmed as a very genuine sort of fellow, and the streak of violence *did* seem irrelevant. What we'd hoped for, of course, was more evidence of a possible association with Shirley, but on that the report offered nothing. Or so we thought. Then, as Noll went through it a second time, he suddenly said, more or less to himself, "Half a minute —San Sebastián . . ." He was studying the list of Jackson's recent deliveries. "I wonder. . . ." He took a file from his desk and ran his finger down another list, comparing the two. It was the schedule of Shirley's own movements, which she'd given to Willie Frost. "Any idea where Monte Gordo is, Linda?" he asked.

I seemed to remember it was in Portugal, but that was all, so I rang the library and they sent someone down with a gazetteer and a map of the Iberian Peninsula, and I looked the place up.

"It's a little resort at the eastern end of the Algarve," I said, "close to Spain. Population practically nothing. Holiday spot, good winter climate." I showed Noll the map.

He gave it a quick glance. "You know," he said, "I think we may be on to something. These two lists have a great deal in common. Take a look."

113

I did—and there was no doubt about it. They tallied in a most intriguing way. What we found was this:

First, Jackson and Shirley were in Tobermory for an overlapping period of several days in early September.

Then, while Shirley was at Saint-Jean-de-Luz, Jackson collected a boat from San Sebastián. Saint-Jean-de-Luz is only a few miles from the French-Spanish border on one side; San Sebastián is only a few miles from it on the other.

Monte Gordo is bang up against the Portuguese-Spanish border. During the period Shirley was there, Jackson did a delivery from Huelva to Gibraltar—and was detained in Huelva with "engine trouble." Huelva is the first sizable port you come to on the Spanish side of the border, and is less than a day's sail from Monte Gordo.

Then Menton. Shirley was there from March 5th to April 9th. During that period, Jackson delivered a yacht from Genoa to Marseilles. A trip that would have taken him past Menton.

Finally, Shirley's few days in Paris on her way home. While she was there, Jackson did a delivery from Ramsgate to Calais. Three hours by train, and he could have been in Paris, too.

Could all that have been coincidental? Of course, if a girl is keen on foreign jobs by the sea, and a man delivers yachts round the coasts of Western Europe, the chances must be high that he'll pass close to the places she's staying at, from time to time. But Saint-Jean-de-Luz and San Sebastián? Monte Gordo and Huelva? How coincidental can you get?

And there are other things that point the same way. Jackson preferring not to carry a crew, for instance. Or if he did have a crew, making sure he had a day or two on his own first, readying the boat. Or a day or two afterward, clearing things up. Then there was his insistence on taking his own time over jobs, never hurrying. And his liking for "looking around." And his choosiness about what deliveries he undertook. And Shirley's choosiness about *her* jobs. And the two convenient engine breakdowns.

It really does look as though there could have been a continuing relationship, of a sort, all through the winter. It wouldn't have been too difficult to arrange meetings. There's always the telephone. Shirley would presumably have had her "time off," and a boat's cabin would make a private and cozy rendezvous.

If there were meetings, were they to do with a plot? Noll thinks not —at least, not at first. He made the point once again that it was unlikely any conspiracy would have started until, for whatever reason, James became a worthwhile target. He thinks that if the pair met, it was as ardent lovers, not conspirators, and that the conspiracy developed only later.

I said I didn't think that four or five meetings over six months indicated exactly a passionate affair, but Noll disagreed. He said it was the quality, not the quantity, that counted (debatable, I thought!), and there might have been reasons why they couldn't meet oftener. He said a man would have to have pretty intense feelings about a woman to organize a series of yacht deliveries in order to meet her. He saw Jackson as a very eager and determined lover, ready to make any effort—like the man who swam the Hellespont. I said that was a fine romantic picture he was drawing, but how about Jackson behaving like some sort of nautical Bill Sikes only a year or so back, threatening to kill some other girl because she'd got tired of him? How did that square with a deep attachment to Shirley? Noll said no one stayed jealous forever, and a year or so was quite long enough for a passionate man to get crazy about someone else— which is no doubt true.

Of course, we may be totally wrong about all this. We're so anxious to pin something on Jackson and Shirley we're straining to make the facts fit. There's still no *evidence* of these supposed lovers' meetings. Only proximity.

It's a weakness, too, that Jackson is genuinely in business. Things would look much more hopeful if he'd *suddenly* taken to seafaring. But, as Noll says, crooks often have genuine businesses to cover nefarious activities. Yacht delivering might seem a bit extreme as a cover job, but perhaps not for a man with a sea background.

We're still floundering, but we're sufficiently encouraged to keep at it.

If only someone would come up with a reasonable motive!

11 P.M.

Someone has!!! A sort of one, anyway.

This evening Noll called together all the reporters who've been working on the case. He said he wanted them to have the complete picture, not just the bits they'd been concerned with, because that way they'd have a better chance of coming up with some useful suggestion. And he gave them a rundown of all our activities and discoveries to date, and his view of the present position.

He ended (I quote my shorthand note):

"So there it is. We have our suspicions. We have some rather disconnected theories about how certain things might have happened. But we don't have anything approaching a case. Perhaps the biggest gap of all is the total lack of any discernible motive. The idea that Shirley Holt's charges could be the result of some peculiar mental disturbance obviously has to be discarded if Jackson is in on it, too. They'd hardly both be disturbed! Then, there's not a scrap of evidence that either of them is interested in politics. Earlier on we were toying with the notion that some ambitious rival of Lester's might have bribed Shirley Holt to make her allegations, but it's hard to take that seriously. Yet one thing's certain: no one would conspire on this level, facing all the publicity and all the risks of exposure, if he didn't foresee an advantage in it of some sort. And frankly, I can't see how anyone could stand to gain anything from what's happened. Not personally and materially . . . The trouble is that time is running out fast. I wouldn't think that anyone would offer odds on Jim Lester being leader of his party in forty-eight hours from now—short of a miracle. . . . Well, any ideas? Any miracles?"

There was a long pause, not at all pregnant. The reporters looked at each other, shrugged a bit, pocketed their notes, and were obviously all

116

set to leave when they got the word. Then George Bromley shuffled in his seat and said diffidently that there *was* something that had struck him. (George is the reporter with the "system" and the colored inks and the "bloody wife.") Noll said "Yes?" encouragingly, and George said it was because of the remark that had just been made about "the odds." Maybe, he said, someone was trying to nobble the horse.

We didn't get it at first, not exactly, and George was asked to explain. He did so—still a bit reluctantly, because he's sensitive about his betting knowledge and activities, especially in front of the Editor. He said, "Well, a couple of weeks ago Jim Lester was the hot favorite to win the election. At Sparkbrooks he was 10–1 on. And the other side were 6–1 against."

Noll began to look interested. "Go on," he said.

George went on. "Well, you were saying, sir, you couldn't see how anyone could stand to gain materially from what's happened. But if someone had backed the government side to win at those odds, he'd be all set now to collect a packet."

Noll said, "Let's get this straight, George. Are you suggesting that someone—Jackson, for instance—might have backed the unpopular side at 6–1 against, and then conspired to turn it into the popular side?"

"It was just an idea," George said. "It's happened with horses."

"Mmm . . . He'd have had to put a good deal on to make the effort worthwhile."

"If he'd put a couple of thousand on," George said, "he'd be pretty sure now of a profit of twelve thousand. Men have strangled their wives for less than that."

There was a lot of laughter, in which everyone joined except George. When it had subsided, Noll said, "Do you happen to know how many firms are running a book on the election?"

George knew—of course. "There are only three big ones. Sparkbrooks, Angus Murray, and Jim Black."

Noll considered. "Well," he said at last, "it's a pretty long shot but we've nothing to lose by asking, have we? We'll get on to them first thing tomorrow. Thanks, George—a good contribution. . . . Now—any other suggestions?"

41

SOURCE. Report to the *Post* by George Bromley on inquiries made at Sparkbrooks, bookmakers. Monday, April 23rd. Morning.

Almost all the bets laid with this firm in the six months preceding April 14th (the date of Shirley Holt's first appearance) were on Lester's party —especially toward the end of the period. Sparkbrooks were quoting odds of 7–1 against the government at one time, with virtually no takers. Since April 14th, bets on the government party have been steadily building up, but I'm told the highest individual stake so far is only £500.

42

SOURCE. Report to the *Post* by Fred Savory on inquiries made at Angus Murray, bookmakers. Monday, April 23rd. Morning.

The highest individual stake on the government party in the twelve months to April 14th was £75. During most of the time, very little interest was being taken. Business has been booming since April 14th, but the highest individual stake is still only £400.

43

SOURCE. Report to the *Post* by William Frost on inquiries made at Jim Black, bookmakers. Monday, April 23rd. Morning.

George Bromley must be psychic. No wonder his racing pays off!

I saw Dave Prentice, who runs the election book at Jim Black's. He was very happy to talk—up to a point. It's a business that thrives on publicity, of course.

I asked him if he'd taken any big bets on the government party in the past twelve months. He said, with a chuckle, it depended on what I meant by "big." I said, well, I'd no particular figure in mind, but anything over a couple of thousand. He said in that case the answer was yes. A certain gentleman had staked—wait for it!—£50,000 on the government party on Friday, April 13th, at odds of 6–1 against.

I nearly fell out of my chair.

"We've been wanting to tell the press all week," Prentice said, "but we couldn't do it without the client's permission and he was a bit doubtful at first—said he'd think it over. This morning, though, he came through on the blower and said he'd no objection as long as his name wasn't mentioned. You're the first to hear."

I said, "But it's incredible. Fifty thousand on an almost certain loser! Didn't you ask him why?"

"No—why should I? If a client wants to back his fancy, that's his affair, not ours—unless he's actually frothing at the mouth, and this one wasn't. Mind you, if some innocent old dear came in and wanted to put her life savings on a three-legged horse, we'd try to talk her out of it. But this bloke knew what he was about and he was obviously loaded—

there was no reason at all why we shouldn't take his money. He gave us a check and it didn't bounce. So there wasn't any problem."

"You'd no objection to the large amount?"

"On the contrary, I was delighted—I felt like giving the fellow a big kiss. There'd been so much money coming in on Lester the odds looked like going through the roof—and then people naturally lose interest. At anything over 12–1 on, the profit's hardly worth the trouble after betting tax. This bet went some way to restoring the balance."

"So now you'll probably be paying him £300,000."

"Well, the shouting isn't quite over yet, but it looks that way at the moment, doesn't it? Not that it'll bother us—we'll still have done very nicely thank you on the whole book."

I said, "Well, I'd certainly like to know who this guy is."

"I'm sure you would. I wish I could tell you."

"Couldn't you give me a clue?"

"Sorry—not a hope."

"Do you never in any circumstances disclose the name of a client?"

"Never," Prentice said. "Not without permission." He grinned. "Except sometimes to the police."

44

SOURCE. Linda Tandy's diary. Monday, April 23rd.

Willie Frost's report has staggered us all. No one really believed that these bookmaker inquiries would produce anything—least of all Noll. Now we face a totally new situation.

James joined us at the office just before noon for an emergency conference. We agreed that if Black's client turned out to be Jackson, the case was as good as over. Not that anyone could imagine Jackson with £50,000 of ready cash, but if he was a crook as well as a yacht deliverer anything was possible. Even if the client wasn't Jackson, the bet was so remarkable in the light of what had happened since that it clearly called for investigation. But *we* couldn't investigate it. George Bromley thought he might be able to get the client's name by some roundabout route over a period of time—but not quickly, and not for sure. Only the police could act right away.

The question was whether the police would step in on the strength of a theory not backed by any solid evidence. James thought they would if they were told to—not otherwise. And the word would have to come from the top. "I'll try to see the Prime Minister," he said, "and put the whole case to him." He gave a rather forced smile. "Even an outgoing Prime Minister has a certain amount of influence!" he said.

James is beginning to look very worn. With no meetings, and his campaign virtually suspended, he's in political limbo. He's still trying to put a brave face on things, but he knows the party crisis is near. It could come tomorrow.

2 P.M.

Well, it seems we're going to get action—and fast. James has just phoned to say the P.M. was deeply interested and agreed at once that there was a *prima-facie* case for investigation. A Chief Superintendent is already on the job.

Could the client be Jackson? We're all holding our breath.

45

SOURCE. Report of Detective Chief Superintendent Crane on
inquiries made in connection with an election bet of £50,000.
Monday, April 23rd. Confidential to Chief Commissioner.

Having ascertained the name and address of the client at Jim Black's,
I called this afternoon on a Mr. Arthur Buckle, of Leigh Barn, Wendover, Bucks.

Buckle is a short, plump man in his early fifties. His appearance is a
little unusual, in that his head looks a size too big for his body. He is
a bachelor and lives alone in an attractive small period house. He is
served domestically by a woman who comes in from a nearby village each
morning. He is well-educated and highly intelligent. His manner is
urbane, his talk persuasive. His voice is pitched rather high. (He is
almost certainly a "queer.") He was wearing sandals, orange slacks, and
a bright green pullover.

He is a dealer in antique furniture and objects. He buys these in the
United Kingdom and on the Continent and ships them to the United
States in container loads. He has been building up this business, on a
single-handed, semi-hobby basis, since he came to Wendover some five
years ago. Before that he was of independent means, but says he became
bored with inactivity. He travels a great deal, particularly around the
U.K. and to America, where he has many contacts. When he is away
from home, he closes his place up. The barn, which gives its name to
the property, is a half-timbered building standing some distance from
the house. It is here that he stores his purchases before export. I had

an opportunity to look over the barn. Its contents, which include almost everything from furniture to fire irons, square in all respects with Mr. Buckle's statements.

When I informed him that I had called in connection with a £50,000 election bet I understood he had made, he was intrigued rather than annoyed. He said yes, he had made such a bet, but why should it be of interest to the police? I said it had struck us as so unusual that we thought we should look into it. He should regard my visit, I said, as no more than a friendly call for information, and of course he didn't have to say anything about it at all if he didn't feel like it.

He looked a bit puzzled, but said he was very happy to talk to a Chief Superintendent, which was a new experience for him—and what exactly was on my mind?

I then asked him if he'd care to tell me why he had bet £50,000 on what at the time had appeared to be a certain loser.

He told me, at considerable length, and most interestingly. It was almost like hearing a philosophy of life.

He said (and I paraphrase freely):

"My experience has been that if you want to make money you must do the opposite of what everyone else is doing. Buy when they're selling and sell when they're buying. Take Victoriana—the sort of stuff I've been storing up in the barn for a long time. What would you have got for a marble-topped washstand with a decorated ewer and basin a few years ago? Practically nothing. What would you have got for a collection of Victorian samplers? Practically nothing. Now they're going mad about such things in New York. The trick is to be ahead of the rest with your judgments. And that applies to Lester. When I made that bet, he was the darling of the country. He'd come up fast and was riding high and everyone was certain he was going to win. So I said to myself, 'Buckle, this is your moment. The mob is on his side, so you're against him.'

"You might think that very rash, Superintendent, but I happen to be interested in politics, as well as in furniture, and I had a hunch about Lester. He seemed to me too clever by half, too smart with an audience, too conceited, too much given to talking over people's heads. Unlike his predecessor, old Arthur Grantley, he seemed to me to lack the common touch. And I thought, Here's a man who could come a cropper once he gets on the hustings. So I put my money on the other man. It might seem crazy to you—perhaps it was by most people's standards—but I enjoy doing rather crazy things. If I'd lost the money, I'd just have written it off to experience. Now it looks as though my hunch was right. Mind you, I never thought he'd turn out such a flawed character as he has—that's his misfortune, and my luck. But I thought he'd lose.

"As for the size of the bet—well, these things are relative. I've got a reasonably flourishing business and I can afford to take chances. And big chances are more fun than small chances. If you bet £50,000, you get a real kick, win or lose. If you bet £5, you don't even bother to look up the result. Not if you're me."

My over-all impression of Buckle is that he is a well-heeled, shrewd, and highly eccentric individual who follows his inclinations and makes his own rules. There are no obvious grounds for further inquiries, though a deeper investigation could conceivably produce a different picture.

46

SOURCE. Linda Tandy's diary. Tuesday, April 24th.

James was shown the report on Arthur Buckle last night, and this morning he came to the office and gave us a confidential summary of it. Reluctantly, we had to agree with his view that the authorities had done all that could be expected of them in the circumstances. The police obviously have to have *some* evidence, *some* grounds, for continuing to question anyone. If they have nothing, it becomes a persecution—and an especially dangerous one when they're acting on political directions from the top. Oh, yes, we all agreed about that—as good citizens. But it doesn't mean we're satisfied. We're not in the least satisfied.

It's fantastic that anyone, however well-to-do and however eccentric, should bet £50,000 on a political party which at the time the bet was made was heading straight down the drain. Whatever reasons Buckle may give, however prejudiced against James he may be, *it simply is not rational* virtually to throw away £50,000, which was what he was doing. And against the background of a possible plot by two other people to rig the election, the bet is more than suspicious. *Could* it be a coincidence that a man stands to gain a cool £300,000 on a turn of events that no one could have foreseen except those who brought it about? I don't believe it. I simply don't believe it.

Buckle is new on the scene and we don't know much about him. We certainly haven't a single item of solid information to link him with the other two. But in one respect he perfectly fills a gap in our tentative theory. It always seemed that Shirley and Jackson lacked the mental caliber, the sophistication, and the political knowledge that would be needed to think up such a grandiose and esoteric ploy. Buckle has all those qualities. With him as the idea man, the trio would be formidable indeed. "The Brains, the Brawn, and the Beauty," as Noll put it.

There are other things that have given us food for thought. For instance, the many similarities in the recent history and way of living of these three. They all seem to have started up their various businesses at about the same time—four to five years ago. In the course of their work they all come in contact with very well-to-do people. They are all basically self-employed—even Shirley, since she takes jobs or not as she wishes (or used to)—which means they've had a large measure of freedom to move around without anyone keeping tabs on them. They're all unmarried, which gives them even greater freedom. They all live alone in their respective establishments. And they all travel a great deal. It would be hard to imagine a more perfect setup for a gang of professional conspirators.

Yet none of this brings us any nearer to clinching the matter. It fills out the theory a little, but we've still no proof of anything. We can suspect Buckle as much as we like—we can even say among ourselves that he *must* be a crook—but how can anyone ever *prove* that his bet wasn't honest and genuine? Of course, if we could show some connection between Buckle and the others, things would be very different. If we could merely find solid and incontrovertible evidence that Shirley knew Jackson—instead of just deducing it—the position would be transformed. But we can't.

If there were time, it might be possible to carry out the superintendent's "deeper investigation" of all the trio—like going back over their earlier history, checking up on them when they were doing other jobs or living on "independent means," perhaps finding some way of looking into their financial transactions, and so on. In the end, we might turn something up. We might even be able to find some point back in time when their lives openly converged, which must have happened if they're now working as a gang. Obviously they'd have had to get to know each other in the first place. But such an investigation would take weeks, perhaps months. And we have only hours.

I'm afraid we now have to face the heartbreaking fact that all our efforts have come to nothing and that we're at the end of the road. Our time has run out, and James can't be saved. Hardly anyone believes in him any longer, except Noll and me. The nation is against him, and so are most of his party. So many people—all out of step with us!

It's a great tragedy—not just for James personally, but for the country. He'd have made a fine Prime Minister. It's almost beyond belief that he may soon be hounded out of public life altogether.

What makes everything so much worse is the feeling that the truth is so nearly within our grasp—that one big heave in the right place could do it. But where is the right place? I've never known Noll to look so frustrated. He's desperate to do *something*—but what?

Later

The word is that the party ax will fall this evening. I don't know whether James intends to fight to the last or not. I would think probably not. He seemed quite crushed today, and beyond the help of anyone.

47

SOURCE. Report in *Evening Star.* From "Our Political Correspondent, Derek Jones." Tuesday, April 24th.

PROGRESSIVES IN CRISIS
A NEW LEADER?

An emergency meeting of the Parliamentary Progressive Party has been called for nine o'clock this evening. Throughout the day, Progressive M.P.s have been contacted by phone and telegraph, and many who had already left for their constituencies are now on their way back to London. No official information has been issued about the purpose of the meeting, but I understand it will review the crisis in the party's affairs arising from the Lester case. Since Miss Shirley Holt first made her allegations about Mr. Lester eight days ago, there has been a catastrophic decline in the party's support throughout the country.

It is almost certain that after discussions, which are expected to last for several hours, a drastic decision will be taken by the emergency meeting. This afternoon a rough-and-ready poll of Progressive M.P.s who were already in London suggested that a large majority have reluctantly come to the conclusion that a new leader must be found.

If, as is likely, Mr. Lester is persuaded to step down in the interests of unity, the veteran Leslie Shirman, who held the office of Home Secretary in the last Progressive administration thirteen years ago, will probably be the party's choice as his successor.

With scarcely more than two weeks to go to polling day, realists in the party have no expectation that public confidence can be sufficiently regained for victory, even under a new leader. They hope, however, that a landslide can be avoided.

48

SOURCE. Linda Tandy's diary. Tuesday, April 24th.

7:30 P.M.

In spite of everything, Noll hasn't given up yet.

He was supposed to be writing the editorial today, our regular leader writer being away ill, but when I went in at six-thirty to see how he was getting on he still hadn't finished it, and Harry Byers, our old head printer, was hovering near the door. Harry always starts hovering for leader copy around six-thirty. He's been with the *Post* for nigh on forty years, and at near-retirement age he should have become philosophical. But his greatest fear is still that one day, because of dilatoriness on high, the leader will miss the first edition and the column will appear blank.

Anyway, Noll was certainly late with his piece—and afterward I realized why. He'd spent the whole afternoon incommunicado in his room, going back over every detail of the case history, all the reports from the boys and everything, and making notes on a pad. Quite brief notes, actually. They ran:

Jackson is crazy about Shirley.
Jackson was threatening to kill some girl.
Jackson had to reberth his boat.
Someone there till dusk.
Fishermen didn't know exact time.
J. has a hell of a temper.
Phone, or go?

It seemed a small mouse from a great mountain of paper, not to mention hours of concentrated work and thought. Naturally I asked Noll what it was all about. He said curiosity killed the cat. *Very* amusing!

He's up to something, that's obvious. He's working late tonight, and he's asked me to stay on, too. Canteen suppers for both. Ugh!

As though suppers matter . . .

7:45 P.M.

A note has just come by hand from James.

49

SOURCE. Note from James Lester to Oliver Tandy. Tuesday, April 24th.

Progressive Party HQ
Smith Square
7 P.M.

Dear Noll and Linda,

I am sending you this note with a heavy heart. I can't go on any longer as I have been doing—the burden is too great, and there are limits to what one can take. Now there is only one thing to do and I must do it, however grievous the consequences to myself. I shall be making a personal statement around midnight, which should catch your later editions.

Thank you both for everything. I wish your faith in me had been better rewarded.

Yours ever,
J.

50

SOURCE. Front page of the *Post.* Wednesday, April 25th.

LESTER CONFESSES!
MIDNIGHT SENSATION
"I LIED"

James Lester, the leader of the Progressive Party, confessed at a press conference called late last night that Shirley Holt did spend a night with him on his yacht. He announced that he was resigning all his public offices and his seat in Parliament, and said he expected to be charged with perjury.

In a voice shaking with emotion, he read out the following statement before a hushed audience:

"I have called you together to tell you that everything I have said during the past week about myself and Miss Shirley Holt has been untrue. Everything that Miss Holt has said is true. I did make her acquaintance on the beach in Mull. I saw her sunbathing there when I emerged from the cabin of my boat shortly after four o'clock in the afternoon. I went ashore and got into conversation with her as she has stated. The rest followed. I did swim naked with her, I did invite her to my yacht, and I did make love to her.

"I lied because I thought it was the only way to prevent the wrecking of my political career. I hoped that my denials would be accepted by the public and that Miss Holt would not press the matter. I thought it would all blow over. I deeply regret having caused her so much pain and distress by my denials.

"I have no excuses to offer. I know that what I have done is unforgivable. A great burden of guilt is on my conscience. Naturally I am giving up all my public offices, including my seat in Parliament. I accept the fact that I am liable to be prosecuted for perjury. I shall take whatever punishment may come without complaint.

"I particularly regret the injury done to my closest friends, whom I have cruelly deceived. There are no grounds on which I can claim their indulgence."

51

SOURCE. Report by Fred Savory to Oliver Tandy. Wednesday, April 25th. Telephoned to the *Post*, 2 P.M.

Having got our Colchester stringer to check last night that Jackson was in residence, we drove down to West Mersea early this morning, arriving just before eight o'clock. We were in my car and I was driving. Willie Frost was beside me, George Bromley occupied two-thirds of the back seat, and John Fletcher was squeezed in next to him. We did a slow run along the front so that John could point out Jackson's barge, and I parked under trees in a side street where we had a good view of the scene without being conspicuous. Jackson's car was on its platform over the saltings. There was no sign of any activity aboard the barge. We settled down to wait. Nothing happened until about nine o'clock, when Jackson emerged in trousers and singlet, sniffed the air, stood for a few moments looking out over the saltings and the channel, and went below again.

By now there was quite a bit of morning traffic on the coast road, mostly trade vans. At nine-fifteen, an Express Dairy man delivered a pint of milk to Jackson, and at twenty to ten a boy delivered his newspaper.

It was just before ten when Jackson came rushing out. He threw himself into his car, narrowly missed a woman on a bicycle as he reversed into the road, and shot off at high speed. I followed.

We managed to keep on his tail without too much difficulty—helped by the fact that we had a pretty good idea where he was going. He took the Colchester-London arterial road as far as the North Circular, then turned west. He was doing a good sixty in the 40 m.p.h. limits (so were we, but fortunately he was in front), and he was flagged down by a stationary police car just short of Finchley. We drifted past and parked in a layby to wait for him. He shot by in about ten minutes. His chat with the police had done nothing for his temper and not much for his speed, but once we were off the North Circular he had to slow for the traffic. He had his own route to Surbiton and we closed up in order not to lose him. He reached Egerton Road just after midday, braked to a squealing halt outside No. 37, and dashed upstairs. We heard a bell ringing, then the sound of a flat door being slammed behind him. We went up as quietly as we could to the top landing.

There was already a furious row going on inside and we didn't need any electronic devices to hear what was being said. Shirley was saying that Jackson must be out of his mind to be calling on her openly like this. Jackson shouted that he didn't bloody well care and that she was an effing little bitch and the paper proved it. There was a moment of comparative quiet—presumably while Shirley looked at the paper. Then, in a high, scared voice, she said it wasn't true, it was all lies. Jackson said *of course* it was true—did she think he was an idiot? Lester would never have said it if it hadn't been true—ruining himself, probably going to jail. She was just a bitch—a randy bitch. Jackson was really working himself up now, not giving her a chance to speak. He said he couldn't have been off the beach for more than ten minutes before she'd got cracking. He said he'd warned her the last time, and this was it.

Shirley began to cry. She kept saying that it wasn't true, none of it was true. Jackson yelled at her, "You're lying, you stinking little whore," and we heard a blow, and Shirley screamed, and there were more blows.

At that point I rang the bell, and the noise stopped, apart from Shirley sobbing hysterically. We waited, knowing there was no way out for Jackson from the top floor except through the flat door. After a moment I rang again, and kept my finger on the bell until the door opened and Jackson looked out. "Who the hell are you?" he said.

We didn't talk, we just went in and grabbed him. He fought like a maniac and it took three of us to get him to the floor and overpower him. He suffered some damage, because we hadn't liked what he'd done to the girl. (We had casualties, too. Willie lost two teeth, John's left eye is closed, and I'll be indenting for a new suit.) Anyway, we got him under in the end, and George Bromley sat on him. Then John phoned the police and I did what I could for the girl. Her face was a pulpy mess —she'd taken a horrible beating in those few seconds.

The police were pretty cooperative from the start, because there was no doubt Jackson had viciously assaulted the girl, who wasn't his wife, so it wasn't even a domestic row, and we had our press cards to show who we were. Then, as soon as I could, I gave them the whole spiel— referring them to Jim Lester, to the Police Commissioner, to you, to the Prime Minister, the lot. If I'd been on my own, they'd probably have thought I was round the bend, but the others backed me up, and it wasn't likely there'd be four crazy newsmen all at once, and the outcome was the cops took Jackson and Shirley off to the local station and the nearest casualty department, respectively, while further inquiries were made.

We're now going along to the station ourselves to make statements while the words we overheard are fresh in our minds.

52

SOURCE. Report by Edith Curtis to Oliver Tandy. Wednesday, April 25th. Telephoned to the *Post*, 2 P.M.

As you'll probably have heard by now, the West Mersea part of the plan worked perfectly and I hope the rest did.

I dropped young Alfie on the coast road at eight-thirty, pointed out the barge to him, gave him the bag of newspapers with the vital one on top, lent him my watch, and told him to make the delivery between nine-thirty and nine-forty-five and then wait round a corner and out of sight until I picked him up.

I then parked my car in the village near the shops, put on a pair of dark glasses, and strolled over to the stationer's. The morning papers had just come in and were being sorted and marked for delivery. After a while the real newsboy turned up and collected his load and set off on his round, and I followed him, also on foot. The first part of the round was away from the seafront, so there was no problem. When he seemed to be working toward the coast road, I stopped him and asked him if he knew where The Lane was, and he said he did and started to give me directions. I said I couldn't see very well, especially going across roads, and if he'd take me to The Lane I'd give him a pound for his trouble. He was a nice little boy, and he said it was no trouble, and he took my arm and conducted me to The Lane, which at my pace was about twenty minutes' walk away. He didn't want to take the pound, but I insisted, and I kept him chatting about his school and how long his Easter holidays lasted and about his family and what he wanted to be when he grew up, and by the time he left to finish his round it was after ten o'clock.

53

SOURCE. Linda Tandy's diary. Wednesday, April 25th.

Oh, what a beautiful morning! Oh, what a beautiful day! Hallelujah! I know I'm not being calm and controlled. I know I'm practically hysterical with happiness. But it's worked! It's worked, and we've won. It's all over, and we've won. I never thought we'd pull it off, but we have. We've got all the proof we need. James is going to be cleared. James is going to be safe. All the doubters are going to be confounded. The whole awful business is finished and we can start to live again.

I have to hand it to so many people—but especially to Noll, toiling upward through the afternoon while the rest of us were preparing to abandon a lost cause. Picking out those vital points—like Jackson having left the beach first, so he couldn't know what happened afterward; and the fishermen not having mentioned a time, so J. couldn't be sure it was *him* and Shirley they'd seen. Then making a pattern of it all, and planning the action. Of course, it was a gamble, as Noll knew very well. So many things could have gone wrong. But we'd nothing to lose if it didn't come off. And the prospects *were* hopeful. It was a near certainty that Jackson would accept the *Post* story at its face value, the power of the printed word being what it is. Who would doubt the genuineness of a factual report with big headlines on the front page of one's own newspaper? And it was a fair bet that a man who'd shown himself as jealous and violent as Jackson wouldn't be content just to phone the

136

girl and shout at her; it would be action he'd want, not chat. Anyway, those were Noll's two main premises, and happily they both turned out right.

Of course, he didn't know then that the girl Jackson had been so furious with a year or so ago was actually Shirley—that was a real bonus —though he says the thought had crossed his mind.

Noll told me about his plan at eight o'clock last night, over canteen coffee, shortly before he briefed the reporters and invited volunteers. He hadn't had a chance to discuss it with James, who at that time was busy preparing the personal statement he planned to make at the meeting of the parliamentary party.

(Incidentally—and that's the right word, because who cares now?— that personal statement, which of course was to have been an announce-ment of resignation, was never made. Apparently James, at the last moment, decided that he'd go down fighting, and he put up such a show and was so emphatic that time would exonerate him, and perhaps very soon, that sufficient M.P.s were uneasy enough to feel they'd like to sleep on the problem. So the meeting was adjourned at midnight without any decision being taken. Now no one will have to worry any more. I bet they're all thankful they waited!)

On the whole, I think it was just as well James *wasn't* in on the plan. That confession piece that Noll concocted was so revoltingly convincing it almost turned *my* stomach. I'm sure James would have hated it.

There were no technical problems to speak of over the phony story. Dear old Harry Byers hung on through the early hours till the machines had stopped rolling, and then he set up the new front page with banner headlines and large type so the confession occupied most of the space, and locked up the new type in the old forms—I think that's what he said; I'm still fairly vague about printing—and then he took two pulls by hand. After that it was just a question of substituting the outside sheets of the phony version for two of the genuine version. The second copy was a spare—just a precaution. Noll says he'll keep the first one as a family heirloom and perhaps offer the other to the Press Club or some museum. Personally I'd sooner they were both burned. I can't bear to look at them.

We had a little celebration at the office this evening, in Noll's room. Just for the leading characters in the counter-conspiracy—and, of course, James. It was pretty hilarious. Noll toasted young Alfie, our "newsboy," who's actually a copy boy—"probably our next editor"; and Harry the printer—"let's hope his union doesn't suspend him for working overtime without pay"; and the reporters—"especially those with missing teeth and black eyes"; and finally James, who for the first time in his life seemed to have difficulty in finding words. But he did say he hoped to see us all for tea in Downing Street!

It's all been such a *bouleversement* that no one is behaving quite normally.

Later

Arthur Buckle has been arrested. He is being held on a charge of fraudulent conspiracy.

Latest

We hear that Shirley Holt is about to tell all.

The Public Prosecutor, James learned, is anxious to get a full picture of the trio's activities, which he thinks may have been going on long before the Lester affair—in which case he might be able to bring other charges and get Buckle and Jackson sent down for a long stretch. The best hope is for Shirley Holt to turn Queen's evidence, with a promise of police protection and no prosecution. Apparently she's completely disenchanted with her boyfriend after having her face bashed in, and is willing to play. Saving her own skin at the end—typical. No remorse, we gather—no real awareness of the enormity of her conduct, or the immense harm she's done to the country. Trying to put a gloss on everything, to make it sound almost innocent. She must lack a moral dimension.

138

It irks one that she should get away with it like this, but I suppose it's the sensible course. Anyway, is she *really* getting away with it? What future can she have?

I can hardly wait to know the whole inside story.

54

SOURCE. Voluntary statement made by Shirley Holt at Surbiton Police Station on Wednesday, April 25th, and Thursday, April 26th.

I met Frank Jackson when I was twenty years old. My mother had just died and had left me some money and I decided to go to Nice for a holiday. I flew, and Frank was sitting next to me in the plane. We talked together all the way, and when we landed we arranged to meet again. We got to know each other quite well in Nice. Frank seemed to have plenty of money, and he was very interested in yachts. He said he had been a sailor at one time but had given it up because there were better ways of making a living. While we were in Nice, he persuaded me to sleep with him. I'd had one or two mild affairs before, but this was the first time I became seriously involved with a man. I found him very attractive.

Soon after we got to Nice, he introduced me to a friend of his, an older man named Arthur Buckle, who was living and working on the Riviera at that time. Frank had met Arthur on a liner when he was on the way out to take charge of some millionaire's yacht in Bermuda, and they'd got to know each other well and eventually formed a sort of partnership. Arthur could be very amusing when he liked, and he seemed to have been all over the world. He was a very sophisticated man.

He was also a queer, so in a sense it may seem strange that Frank got on with him, because Frank was anything but that. In fact, they were quite opposites. Frank was a little bit on the rough side, at times, but he was very masculine and very forceful, which I suppose was why he appealed to me so much. At that time, at any rate. He had a great respect for Arthur's brains, and Arthur admired Frank as a practical man—one who was reliable in a tight corner and wouldn't stand any nonsense from anyone. So they got on well together and had a good business relationship.

After a while they suggested I should go into the partnership, too, because I could help a lot if I was there as Frank's "fiancée"—there are so many things a girl can do more easily than a man. And I did, and the business flourished more than ever. I know that what we were doing wasn't exactly legal, in the strictest sense, and that some people might call it blackmail; but it wasn't really that, because if we did happen to learn something about a person to his discredit we never actually asked for money. We always said that the secret was safe with us and we'd no intention of telling anyone—so if we were given presents it was out of gratitude, which is quite different. Frank was once given a very large present after he'd found out that a boat he was delivering was being used for smuggling—and he never threatened to tell anyone. And there was an American senator who was very grateful because we promised not to tell his wife about an affair he was having with an airline stewardess. We certainly never wanted to cause any trouble; we were most scrupulous about that.

Anyway, as I say, the business was flourishing. In fact, it was doing so well that Arthur started to get nervous. Of course, we weren't staying in any one place: we were moving around all the time, and often quite fast. But Arthur said that if we went on meeting openly and doing lots of jobs, the police were sure to catch up with us, and they'd want to know who we were and where we lived and what we lived on. In fact, all about us—and we wouldn't have adequate answers. He said that what we needed were three respectable cover jobs—preferably jobs where we

would be meeting well-to-do people and making useful new contacts—
and that we should lie low for a time and only get together in secret.
He said he rather fancied going into the antiques business himself, being
the arty-crafty type, and he thought I would be perfect as a high-class
children's nurse. Frank wasn't too keen on that idea, because he couldn't
see how he and I would be able to get together for fun and games if I
was tied up with small children. Arthur didn't think there'd be any
problem, because everyone had time off, and I could try and get jobs at
seaside places, and if Frank did something with boats, which was obviously his line and which he enjoyed, we could meet quite easily. Frank
still wasn't convinced, because what he really wanted to do was settle
down and be with me all the time; he was actually quite crazy about me.
But Arthur said he wasn't proposing this scheme as anything more than
a temporary thing; his idea was that we should have a sort of fallow
period, and meanwhile try to think up some really brilliant ploy which
would bring us all a big fortune and allow Frank and me to retire and
marry if we wanted to. This appealed to Frank very much, and he had
a lot of faith in Arthur, and in the end he agreed to go along with the
plan and set up as a yacht deliverer, which he knew he could do.

Well, things didn't work out too badly to start with. We were able
to talk to each other quite freely on the phone, because with S.T.D.
nobody can listen in, and Frank and I managed to meet fairly often,
sometimes on one of his boats and sometimes in a quiet spot like the
beach at Tobermory, but always very carefully and secretly. Frank had
a list of my engagements well in advance and he often managed to
arrange his own schedule to fit in with it, or if that wasn't possible he'd
come by car when he was free and pick me up. He'd ring me beforehand,
or I'd ring him, and we'd fix exactly where we'd meet and when, so there
was no problem there. And there was no problem about my free time,
either, because I almost always had the evenings to myself after the
children were in bed, and usually a whole free day each week as well.
And sometimes, as at Tobermory, there was a gap between my engagements, and then we could have several days together. It was actually

rather fun, planning and arranging, and knowing that it was all happening without anyone else having a clue what was going on.

We were none of us short of money during this time, because in addition to what we were earning we had all managed to put something by—though not in banks, of course. Arthur had the most, because he'd been in business longest, and by now his antiques were beginning to do quite well and bring in money in the ordinary way. And every now and then he'd come up with some little idea—nothing ambitious but enough to keep us in training, you might say—and that would top up the reserves. We would arrange our affairs so that we had time to carry it out, whatever the scheme was.

At first I didn't go abroad much because I wasn't sufficiently well known and didn't get the top opportunities. But gradually the overseas jobs increased, and I did rather like them, and Frank began to get very restive. He's always been jealous, and whenever we met he'd ask me about the people I'd got to know and especially about men. I pointed out that with small children to look after I didn't have much chance to get to know other men even if I'd wanted to—which was true, really. But there was one occasion near Le Havre when I met a rather nice French boy and I went out with him in his car a few times, and we did have a sort of quick affair—well, one gets a bit lonely—and unfortunately Frank was a day early for a meeting we'd fixed, and by pure chance he actually saw me getting out of this boy's car and being kissed good night, and then there was the most furious row you could imagine. Frank wouldn't believe the thing had stopped at kissing—and of course it hadn't, though I never admitted it. Still, he knew—it's odd how one does know these things—and I thought he'd never forgive me. I promised that nothing of the sort would ever happen again, and he said it had better not because he'd break my neck if it did. He had to go off then, but in a week or two he'd cooled down and was ringing me again to make another arrangement.

It was after this incident that Frank started to needle Arthur about that big idea that was going to make all our fortunes and allow Frank and me to settle down together in luxurious retirement.

Well, of course, big ideas don't come fully shaped out of anyone's head, even one as clever as Arthur's, but it *was* he who started the thing off. You see, he happens to know about politics. He's really interested, goodness knows why, and he was having a phone talk with Frank a few weeks ago, just a general sort of chat, and he happened to mention Jim Lester and how he'd suddenly sprung into prominence—which naturally interested him, because it's usually only the prominent people like senators and tycoons and so on who have much to offer in our line of business. Frank then said that he'd actually *met* Lester at Tobermory back in the autumn when he and I were keeping one of our dates, and that he'd had several long talks with him and a few drinks and so on. Arthur was interested and asked for more details, and Frank told him about Lester's yachting holiday and how the man he was with had been called away and how he'd seen his boat anchored offshore when we were sunbathing on a beach one afternoon and how Lester had tried to get to Oban that night and couldn't make it, and how I'd stayed at a motel where I could come and go easily. Naturally Frank didn't come out with all this right away; these things hadn't meant anything to him at the time any more than they had to me, and he had to go back in his memory a good bit. It was Arthur who kept putting questions to him, trying to get the whole picture.

The next day they talked again, after Arthur had had time to think about it, and on this occasion Arthur had a lot more questions to ask —a whole long list of them and much more detailed. He wanted to know just how much Frank could remember about the inside of Lester's boat, which turned out to be quite a lot, and how far offshore Lester had anchored, and how long he'd stayed there, and what the beach was like, and whether anyone else had been around, and when we'd left. He wanted to know exactly what Lester had said to Frank about his attempted night passage when he got back. He wanted to know the exact setup at the motel. In fact he wanted to know everything. Arthur is a very thorough man.

It was only after he'd got the answers to all his questions and done a bit more thinking that he outlined a sort of plan which involved me.

It wasn't so very different from things we'd done before, except that it was more complicated. Frank said the idea was ingenious and could work, but where was the money in it, where was the fortune, because Lester wasn't an oil millionaire, like some people we'd known, and anyway he wasn't likely to pay anyone to keep quiet about something he hadn't done. Then Arthur told Frank about his betting plan, which was brilliant and something Frank wouldn't have thought of in a thousand years.

Well, the two of them went on working things out for a bit, and then Frank phoned me in Menton and we arranged to meet in Paris, which was convenient for one of his deliveries, so he could put me in the picture. I didn't have anything against the plan in principle because it wasn't as though I was going to accuse Lester of any crime, and anyway politicians aren't exactly honest themselves, are they, and if his side lost the election the other side would win, and what was the difference? But I was much more doubtful on other grounds. For one thing I wasn't sure of being able to act the part, which would be much more difficult and would last longer than anything I'd done before, and I'd have to be constantly on my guard in case I was tripped up by some awkward question. And in general I thought the whole plan full of risks. But Frank said he and Arthur had considered all the risks very carefully—and he mentioned several that they'd thought about. For instance, he said, there was no chance that anyone would remember seeing me at the motel that night, because of the cafeteria setup and meals not going on the bill. There was no chance that anyone would be able to confirm Lester's story about his night passage attempt, because boats always gave each other a wide berth at night. There was no chance that anyone could have seen Lester's boat anywhere but off the beach, since I'd stayed there myself till quite late and it had still been at anchor when I'd walked back to the motel along the cliff in the dusk. In fact there wasn't any risk at all, because whatever Lester said no one could *prove* that my story wasn't true. All I had to do was keep on saying the same thing, and if there were any awkward questions about things I didn't know about, just say I couldn't remember, which would be fair enough after a gap of seven months. I said what about the bet—would people believe that it was a genuine gamble? Frank said the point was that nobody could possibly *prove* it wasn't, so the £300,000 or thereabouts was safe and easy money, and he and I would certainly be able to retire on our two-thirds share.

By now, I was more than half convinced, but I said that to make the story stick I thought we ought to have a bit of solid evidence that I'd known Lester and been on his boat. Frank said he could tell me so much about the boat, and about Lester himself, that no more evidence would be needed—but I wasn't so sure. I said it would be much better if something could be found on the boat that proved I'd been there. Frank said, "Like what?" And I thought for a bit and remembered my ring with the loose stone that I'd been carrying about in my bag and still had with me, and I suggested I could have lost the stone on the boat. Frank thought about that, and when I said the obvious place would be down the washbasin pipe, he said that was quite an idea and he might be able to fix it. He asked me when I'd last worn the ring, and I thought a bit more and said it was while I was with the family at Tobermory, just before they'd left, so that was all right. Frank was quite sold on the idea now, but he said everything depended on where the boat was. He said he'd find out and do a reccy, and phone me at the flat the day I got back to London. He said that in any case Arthur would place his bet, because the topaz thing was an extra and not vital, and I finally agreed to the bet. So then we were committed, because we'd either got to go ahead with the plan and make it work or lose the £50,000 stake.

I arrived home about eleven o'clock on the morning of the thirteenth and Frank phoned within half an hour. He was very excited about what he'd discovered, because he'd located the boat and been to look around the previous night and found it quite easy to approach, and though the boat was all shut up he'd thought of a way of getting the stone into the pipe from the outside if I would squeeze through a gap that was too narrow for him, and Lester wouldn't have any answer at all and he'd be sunk. So that night Frank picked me up near the flat and drove me to Walton and he'd lodged the stone in the end of a rubber tube and all I had to do was blow through it and the stone popped out like a pea from a peashooter. There was absolutely no difficulty at all.

We were all set now, except for a final briefing by Arthur. He rang me in the morning and went over every last detail with me about what I had to do. He said that Lester was speaking at a meeting in the afternoon, and told me the paper where I could say I'd seen the announcement that morning. He said it was a private meeting for members and that I wouldn't be allowed in, but that there would be plenty of other people going in, including probably pressmen, and that if I could get one of them to carry a message, that would almost certainly start things off. He told me just what to say in the message, about the holiday and the sunbathing and so on, and to give my name and address, and then the newspapers would be after me. He said I should be quite casual about it all to start with, and then let the story come out bit by bit as I was asked questions, and not volunteer anything unless I was asked, and in particular I shouldn't hurry about bringing up the topaz thing, because it would keep and someone was sure to give me a natural opening at some stage. Which was just what happened. And he told me I could forget the peculiar name of the boat, because that would seem more reasonable than not, and that in general it was better to remember too little than too much.

Everything went very well to start with. Arthur was in touch with me and with Frank every day by phone, discussing the progress of the plan and the next moves—and he was really very clever about things we wouldn't have thought of. For instance, he said Frank should back up Lester as far as he could to begin with, particularly about the drooping flag on the motor cruiser, because the one thing we didn't want was for Lester to have to resign too soon and let in somebody else, who might get the party on its feet again in time to win the election. All the same, we were a bit worried about that cruiser, because no one had foreseen

146

that Lester might have made close contact with somebody in the dark as a result of some bad navigation. Then other things began to go wrong. A bad mistake was mentioning the ship in the bottle, but no one had thought for a moment that Lester could have bought it so recently. And we'd forgotten all about the fishing boat, which hadn't meant anything to us at the time and which we'd only vaguely noticed. Another problem that arose was whether or not Frank should talk to the *Post* a second time about his yacht delivering, because of the possibility that some bright person might link up his movements with mine. But Arthur decided that if Frank clammed up and refused to talk, that would seem more suspicious than if he was quite open about everything. Arthur still said that whatever suspicions might arise, nobody could *prove* any connection, since Frank and I hadn't been seen together for years, and that it would take more than suspicion to bring in the law, or undo the bet.

In fact, we *would* have been all right if the *Post* hadn't printed that phony front page, which was a very dishonest trick in my view; and if Frank hadn't gone berserk (really because of the French boy) and come rushing over to Surbiton. It was Frank who ruined everything, by being so jealous, and completely deaf to all reason.

I never want to see Frank again. I was very fond of him at one time—in fact I suppose you could say I was infatuated with him and totally under his influence—but that was before I knew how brutal he could be. After what he did to me yesterday, I'd always be terrified of him.

I'm sorry about all the fuss there's been, but I can't see that anyone has been seriously harmed. I'd call it a storm in a teacup myself.

55

SOURCE. A note from James Lester to Oliver Tandy, with enclosure.
Friday, April 27th. Delivered by hand.

Dear Noll,

There was an airmailed letter from Greece in my post at the House last night. Enclosed is a translation I had done this morning. Ironical, isn't it? How we'd have welcomed it a week ago! Not, I think, that it would have been accepted as *absolute* proof, but it certainly would have helped.

As ever,

Jim

Enclosure

Apartment 8
1231 King George V Road
Athens

Honorable Sir,

I was mentioning in my yacht club this week a voyage which I made with some friends last summer in my motor vessel *Eleusis*. This voyage was from Piraeus to the Islands of Orkney and back to Piraeus. I was speaking of the very beautiful waters in the west part of Scotland and the color of the hills in September, and a yachting colleague asked me if I had seen an advertisement by an English Member of Parliament in our newspaper *Elefteria*, which I had not, and he found a copy of the paper and showed it to me. When I reached home, I examined my records and saw that my vessel had been passing through your Sound of Mull during the night of September 5th last. I could recall no close encounter myself, as I was entertaining my guests at a party to celebrate an affiancing, but on being shown your advertisement my skipper was able to recall such an incident late in the night with a small yacht showing very poor lights. This is as much as I can tell you. I write to you as a fellow yachtsman and I hope the information will be of service. I wish you many pleasant voyages, including a long and safe one on the high seas of politics.

Your respectful servant,

Hector Sofianopoulos

56

SOURCE. Linda Tandy's diary. Friday, April 27th.

James rang me up this afternoon. He asked me if I'd be willing to sit on the platform at his meeting at Rugby tonight. It was his first meeting since the trouble ended, and he said he was feeling nervous and would be glad of my moral support. So of course I said I'd be delighted to back him up, and he collected me about six and we drove up the M 1 to Rugby.

It was an absolutely packed meeting; there wasn't an inch of standing room left, let alone seats. I went on to the platform with a few of the local party bigwigs, and the chairman followed with James. As soon as he appeared, everybody got up and cheered like mad. It was what the papers call a standing ovation, and it went on for ages. A day or two before, a lot of the same people would happily have torn James to pieces, but I still couldn't help being moved by the applause.

I must say James didn't *seem* nervous. He said nothing at all about what had happened—not a word. He went straight into a political speech as though there'd been no break at all in his campaign. And he had another great ovation afterward. He's riding the crest of the wave now; with the revulsion of feeling that's taken place, he's certain of victory.

It was after ten when we set off back to London. James said I must be feeling hungry, and he'd laid in a few cold bits and a bottle of Bollinger and would I care to join him in a late supper? I murmured something vaguely affirmative and the next thing I knew we were at his flat in Brook Street, which is a quite super place, and he was pouring the drinks and saying "Cheers."

We sat down, James opposite me, very sedate. He drank a little champagne and put his glass down, and then he sat examining the nails of his left hand as though he'd got a splinter in one of them. Men are really quite extraordinary. For a whole week he'd been fighting for his political life, suffering every sort of indignity, having things thrown at him, being rescued by the police from howling mobs—and he'd taken it all in his stride. Now that he wanted to say something to me, he had to examine his nails.

Finally, he did manage to get a word or two out. "I think we shall win now," he said. "The public are very fickle but at the moment they seem to be on my side. I think I shall be the next Prime Minister."

I said there wasn't a shadow of doubt about that.

He said, "I don't suppose I'll do the job any better than anyone else, but I'm looking forward to having a try." He was silent for a moment. Then he said, "One has to plan ahead a little. I wondered if you'd consider being my hostess."

I said, cautiously, "Well, I'm very flattered, James. I can see you *will* need a hostess. But I do have a job, which I'm rather attached to. What would it involve?"

He said, in his offhand sort of way, "Oh, you'd have to live at Number 10, of course."

I said, "James, circumlocution is something I've never associated with you. What are you trying to say?"

He said, "Well, I'm really asking you to marry me. I've wanted to for a long time but—I didn't know whether I should. After all, I'm old enough to be your father—well, not quite, unless I'd been *very* precocious—but still much older. And then there was Mary—you know I loved her very much. I thought that might be a sort of barrier. And then, lately, I thought perhaps it wouldn't necessarily be a barrier, because if a man loves a woman very much, and he loses her, he's still the same sort of man; he can often love someone else just as much. So I decided to ask you."

I didn't answer him for a moment. What I *wanted* to say was "You silly stupid man, don't you realize that I've adored you for years and dreamed about you night after night and ached to have your arms around me and worried about you and admired you and suffered with you and cried about you and now all I want to do is throw myself at your feet and say over and over again that I love you, I love you?"

That's what I wanted to say, but we all have our pride, and after being so stupid he really didn't deserve all that at once.

So I said, "Of course I'll marry you, James. I've always quite liked you."

73 74 75 76 10 9 8 7 6 5 4 3 2 1